C000092073

The Other Mrs. Champion

Brenda Adcock

Yellow Rose Books

Port Arthur, Texas

Copyright © 2011 by Brenda Adcock

All rights reserved. No part of this publication may be reproduced, transmitted in any form or by any means, electronic or mechanical, including photocopy, recording, or any information storage and retrieval system, without permission in writing from the publisher. The characters, incidents and dialogue herein are fictional and any resemblance to actual events or persons, living or dead, is purely coincidental.

ISBN 978-1-935053-46-0

First printing 2011

9 8 7 6 5 4 3 2 1

Cover design by Donna Pawlowski

Published by:

Regal Crest Enterprises, LLC
4700 Highway 365, Suite A, PMB 210
Port Arthur, Texas 77642

Find us on the World Wide Web at
http://www.regalcrest.biz

Printed in the United States of America

Acknowledgements

I wish I could say where this story came from, but I can't. One day it was just there. Four days and nights later the first draft was completed, although certainly not finished. I have to thank those who read the initial version: Sandy Thornton, Gail Robinson. I honestly can't remember who else might have read it, but thanks from the bottom of my heart. My memory isn't what it used to be. My thanks to Mavis Applewater and her wife, Heather, for answering my questions about same-sex marriage in Massachusetts, and to Carsen Taite and her wife, Lainey, for answering questions about Canadian same-sex marriages. I hope one day Cheryl and I are fortunate enough to become legally married, somewhere, as well.

A special thanks to Donna Pawlowski for a great cover and to my editor, Patty Schramm, for slapping me gently around from time to time. But without my publisher, Cathy LeNoir and Regal Crest Enterprises, there would be no story. Thanks simply isn't enough, but it's all I have at the moment.

A special thank you to the women who read my stories. I hope you continue to enjoy them and they bring a smile to your beautiful faces.

To Cheryl –

For making the sun shine when I'm having a rainy day.

Chapter One

DISTANT, PERSISTENT CHIMING etched its way into Sarah Champion's consciousness, seeming to grow closer and louder, until she realized the irritating noise interrupting her sleep was not her alarm clock. She blinked into the darkness of her bedroom and glanced at the glowing red numbers on the clock. Three in the morning. Who would be ringing her doorbell in the middle of the night? Kelley hadn't called to say she would be flying in early, and the children both had keys. She pressed the button to the front door intercom and cleared her throat. "Hello?" she croaked.

"Sarah? Sarah! It's Walter. I have to speak to you." She barely recognized the cracked and strained voice coming through the call box.

"Walter? Is something wrong?" A knot formed in Sarah's chest. "I'll be down in a minute," she said as she pressed the button to unlock the front door of the Boston Back Bay brownstone. She slid her feet into her slippers and picked up her robe, tying the belt as she made her way down the staircase to the first floor.

She walked into the front room as Walter swallowed the last of what appeared to be a snifter of brandy. Sarah brushed her fingers through her sleep-disheveled, dark blonde hair. "What's wrong, Walter?" she asked.

"You may want to have a seat, Sarah," Walter Blomquist, Kelley's attorney for over thirty years, said, his voice serious. He was as impeccably dressed as always, despite the early hour, but Sarah noticed a slight look of apprehension in his eyes.

"I'm fine," she said, resting a hip against the padded arm of the large sofa facing the fireplace.

Walter cleared his throat and took a deep breath. "I just got off the phone with a Dr. Gilgannon, a neurologist at St. Paul's Hospital in Vancouver."

The mention of Vancouver brought Sarah fully awake. "Has something happened to Kelley? Has she been in an accident?" Sarah felt her body slide to the front of the sofa. She struggled to keep her voice steady and not jump to conclusions.

"Kelley's suffered a massive stroke," Walter said softly. "She's in the Intensive Care Unit at St. Paul's."

Sarah's hand flew to her mouth and tears filled her eyes. "Is she...is she...," she tried.

"She's on life support and hasn't regained consciousness. We need to get there as soon as possible."

Sarah closed her eyes, allowing a single tear to fall onto her cheek. Myriad glimpses of Kelley, her partner and lover of twenty-five years, floated across her mind.

"The corporate jet is being fueled, and a pilot is standing by," Walter said. "I have to stop at my office to pick up some papers and will send the car back for you."

"I need to call Carl and Cherish." Sarah tried to stand, but her legs refused to support her, and she slumped to the floor wracked by inconsolable sobbing. She covered her eyes with her hands as the finality of what was happening a continent away swept through her. Kelley had been her life for so long. It had been less than a month since Sarah kissed her goodbye at Logan International Airport in Boston. Sarah grasped Walter's arms as he helped her back onto the sofa and gathered her in his arms to comfort her.

"I'll contact the children," Walter said softly.

SARAH WASN'T SURE what clothing she had packed into her suitcase as the co-pilot removed it from the trunk of the car and carried it to the baggage compartment of the private airplane. Sarah's body was still numb and her brain felt as if it was drowning. She knew her eyes were red and puffy from crying, but made no attempt to hide her grief.

"Mom? Mom?" her daughter called to her.

"Hm. What?" Sarah stared vaguely at the young blonde standing next to her. When had Cherish grown from a spunky ten-year-old into a married woman of thirty-five with a child of her own? Surely time had not flown by so quickly that Sarah would forget. Strong hands gripped Sarah's upper arms. "Mom! The pilot wants us to board."

Sarah nodded. She hadn't wanted Cherish to accompany her on the heartbreaking journey, but the young woman had insisted. Her daughter had never been fond of Kelley and stubbornly refused to accept their relationship even after two decades. She couldn't imagine why Cherish was so determined to make the trip. Sarah barely remembered Cherish's hurried arrival at the brownstone or her daughter helping her pack and dress for the journey. Why couldn't she think? Kelley was hovering at death's doorstep and needed her to be strong. Kelley was always the strong one, Sarah's rock since the first day they met.

Northridge, Massachusetts, Mid-June, 1984

"SARAH TURNER," THE receptionist called out over the

noise of nearby construction after glancing at the clipboard in her hand.

Sarah jumped at the sound of her name and stood. She tried to calm her nerves by brushing her hands along the sides of her skirt, looking down to make sure her clothing hadn't wilted in the early, humid Massachusetts summer. It had been nearly ten years since she had applied for a job and five years since she was last employed. She attempted a pleasant look, but her lips felt abnormally dry and stiff. She hoisted her purse onto her shoulder and followed the harried and impatient looking secretary down a carpeted hallway. The secretary stopped in front of a partially opened conference room door and tapped on it lightly with her fingernails.

Sarah shifted her weight from one foot to the other and back again. For the second time in less than ten minutes she was startled when the door snapped open. Short brown hair framed the angular face and prominent cheekbones of the woman who greeted her. Her face bordered on the severe, but that was broken by an engaging and comfortable sparkle in her eyes. Soft, intelligent, brown eyes twinkled behind round glasses in thin, pewter-colored frames. She wore dark slacks and a long-sleeved, pastel green Oxford shirt with a buttoned-down collar. Her comfortable-looking black loafers made Sarah yearn to be out of her own high heels. Taller than Sarah by a few inches, the woman extended her hand.

"Mrs. Turner? I'm Kelley Champion and I'll be conducting your interview today. Please come in, and make yourself comfortable. I hope the construction noise doesn't bother you. Deadlines, you know." Kelley gestured toward a padded chair near her own seat at a large conference room table centered in the middle of the room. "You'll have to excuse the table. It can be a little intimidating," Kelley apologized.

"No. It's fine, Ms. Champion."

Kelley sat and leaned back in her chair as she looked over Sarah's application. "What position in particular are you interested in, Mrs. Turner?"

Sarah cringed. She wished she didn't have to be referred to as Mrs. Turner. When she finally worked up the courage to tell Clifford Turner to take a hike, she toyed with the idea of taking back her maiden name. In the end, her mother convinced her it would be too confusing for the children to suddenly have a mother with a last name different from their own. Children didn't need to be burdened with having to explain the failure of their parents to live together any longer.

"I'm willing to train for any position I might be qualified for, Ms. Champion," Sarah answered. She watched as Kelley flipped through several pages before turning her attention back to her.

"Apparently, it's been a while since you were last employed," Kelley said as her eyes shifted up to look at Sarah.

"Yes. After my son was born we decided it would be better for me to stay home. My income was only a secondary one."

"And now you and your husband have a need for additional income once again?"

"No. Now there is no husband. My income will be our only source of money other than child support payments."

Kelley nodded and glanced back at the paperwork. "How many children do you have, Sarah?"

The friendliness in Kelley's voice surprised Sarah. The way she said Sarah's name, softly, gently, felt like a caress. "Two," she answered, forcing her mind back to the matter at hand. "My daughter is ten and my son is five."

"I imagine having to leave them will be difficult for you."

"Perhaps at first, but I'm willing to do whatever I have to in order to provide for them. I'm a hard worker, Ms. Champion, and I learn fast. I have some secretarial skills and know I can learn whatever I have to. My children understand why I need to return to the work force."

Kelley set the application folder on the table and flipped it closed. "The only position we have available for someone at your...skill level would be in our customer service department."

"You mean lack of skills," Sarah said with a grin.

"You have a very pleasant voice, Mrs. Turner. Most of the calls to customer service involve a complaint and the callers are usually unhappy. I'm sure the sound of your voice would calm them down immediately. I personally find it quite soothing to the ear."

"And I'm quite sure my children would have to disagree with you." A twinkle sparkled in Sarah's eyes for the first time since she arrived at the new Bilt-Rite Home Center in the Boston suburb.

"When would you be able to start?" Kelley asked.

"Today! Immediately!" Sarah said.

Kelley pushed her glasses up on the bridge of her nose. "I appreciate your enthusiasm, but the store won't officially open for a couple of weeks. We're just filling a few final jobs and stocking the shelves until then."

"I can stock shelves," Sarah volunteered. "I really need to start work as soon as possible, Ms. Champion." Sarah didn't want to sound desperate, but the truth was she had less than a hundred dollars in her bank account. Even though her ex-husband earned a significant salary as an investment analyst, he was frequently delinquent in making his child support payments. It was difficult to explain to Cherish and Carl why they suddenly didn't have the money to buy even the necessities. At best, she figured she had enough food in the house to last almost a week.

"Stocking is only a temporary position," Kelley explained. "It does require some strenuous lifting." Her eyes drifted over Sarah's body.

"I'm much stronger than I look," Sarah said defensively.

"You'll be spending the next several evenings reading packets about Bilt-Rite so you'll be familiar with our customer service policies, as well as attending in-store training sessions probably next week. I suppose you could stock in the evenings and, hopefully, still have the energy left to sit through what I assure you are sessions specifically designed, at great expense, to put you to sleep."

"That would work out wonderfully," Sarah said.

"Yes. I suppose it would. If you don't mind my asking, who will be watching your children?"

"My next door neighbor has agreed to watch them for me over the summer. I'll make other arrangements when school starts in the fall. My son will begin kindergarten then."

Kelley leaned back in her chair again and rubbed her eyes under her glasses. She readjusted them slightly. "Then I suppose you may consider yourself hired, Mrs. Turner. I'll send the appropriate paperwork to human resources."

The joy on Sarah's face was indescribable. Kelley hoped she wasn't making a mistake. Even if she was, it wouldn't be the first time she had misjudged someone when hiring. But somehow she knew she was making the right decision by hiring Sarah Turner. If nothing else, she was sure she would be checking in on the cute little blonde with the sparkling green eyes from time to time.

"WE'VE BEEN CLEARED by the tower," Walter said, snapping Sarah back from the past. A cool breeze had begun blowing, ruffling Sarah's hair as she nodded and readjusted her purse on her shoulder. She didn't want to go up the steps into the airplane.

"You okay, Mom?" her son, Carl, asked when he appeared next to her.

"No, but I'll do the best I can to fake it," she answered.

"Turn off that damn cell phone, Cherish," Carl told his sister who was standing at the bottom of the plane's steps. "We're boarding."

She waved him off with her hand and ended her call. "I was just checking on Ethan. Nathan's trying to explain to him what's happened to Kelley. It's not like she's his real grandmother or anything, but for some reason he likes her."

Sarah stopped dead in her tracks and turned to face her daughter. "Kelley's been as much a grandmother to Ethan as I have, and it didn't have anything to do with whether she was related to him or not," she snapped. "You're thirty-five years old. Please remember everything Kelley has done for you the last twenty-five of those years even though she knew you hated her. Grow up, for God's sake. I could soon be losing the love of my life, and you're still worried about what people will think if they learn you have two women as parents. In case you've forgotten, Kelley and I are legally married."

"Only in Massachusetts," Cherish shot back. "Everywhere else, you're still a..."

"Come along, Sarah," Walter said gently, guiding Sarah away from the scene of another potentially nasty argument with her daughter.

"I don't know why she insisted on coming with us. She hates Kelley so much," Sarah groused as she felt the tears building in her eyes for the hundredth time since Walter's middle of the night visit. She hated the thought of Kelley being alone in a foreign country. *She must feel so scared and abandoned. Now she's waiting for me, and I won't let her see me as weak.*

Sarah settled into her seat next to the window and adjusted her seat belt. Walter shoved his briefcase into the overhead compartment and unbuttoned the jacket of his suit as he sat in the seat across from her.

While they waited for the co-pilot to close and lock the door, Sarah leaned over to Walter. "Thank you for coming with me, Walter."

He patted her hand. "As Kelley's attorney, I had to come. I have all of her directives and will with me. It was her request in case something should happen to her away from home. As her friend for three decades, it will be like losing a member of my family."

"I never would have dreamed I could be so happy when we met twenty-five years ago."

"Kelley Champion has always been an exceptional woman, Sarah. She was lucky to find someone just as special to share her life."

Northridge, Massachusetts, Early July, 1984

SARAH FELT LUCKY from the first moment she met Kelley Champion. Not only was she hired for a job, but Kelley made her transition back into the work world pleasant and smooth. Although Sarah didn't see Kelley often, it was usually just enough to catch a glimpse of her lop-sided grin from a distance. Kelley had a way of making people feel important and cared about. When anyone spoke to her, her soft brown eyes never left theirs. Once the store opened, the height of Sarah's week came to be Wednesday afternoons. Until a permanent manager for the Northridge store was trained, Kelley would remain as the interim manager. Wednesday afternoon was the day she stopped by to check on how things were going in the Customer Service Department. Even though Sarah rarely had a chance to speak to Kelley, she could feel her presence by the way everyone relaxed when she was around.

Sarah was dealing with a customer complaint the first week of business concerning a product that wasn't a part of the Bilt-Rite inventory. She had been unable to convince the gentleman the product was not theirs and her patience was beginning to wear thin. On her fourth attempt a shadow fell across her desk. She glanced up in time to see Kelley standing next to her, dressed casually as usual. Kelley reached down and gently lifted the telephone headset from Sarah's head. She held the earpiece to her own ear and said, "This is Kelley Champion, the store manager. What seems to be the problem today?"

Kelley listened, occasionally smiling down at Sarah. After the customer's lengthy complaint, she winked at Sarah. "Sir, I'm terribly sorry to tell you, as I'm sure our customer service representative has, that Feldspar is not a product line carried by Bilt-Rite Home Centers." Before the customer could interrupt into another tirade, she continued. "In fact, the primary reason we have chosen not to handle that particular product is because of complaints such as yours. However, the direct number to Feldspar International is 1-800-555-2727. I heartily suggest you contact them directly. Please feel free to come by our new store and let us acquaint you with our brands, which we believe are far superior to the Feldspar products. Thank you for calling and have a wonderful day."

Sarah looked at Kelley in amazement as she disconnected. "You know the number for Feldspar International by heart?"

"I don't have a clue what it is," Kelley said, handing the headset back to Sarah. "But the numbers 2-7-2-7 on the dial spell crap and I figured that would be close enough."

Sarah burst into a hearty laugh and was still smiling when she gave Kelley a small wave as she exited the office.

A week later the staff was informed the permanent store manager would begin the following week. Sarah wasn't quite sure why the news made her a little sad. The other secretaries told her Kelley Champion was really an opener. Her primary job was to make sure new stores in the Bilt-Rite franchise opened either on time or ahead of the projected schedule. That required she hire all staff and make sure the new store's inventory was in place and fully stocked before the arrival of the permanent manager.

Kelley's final Wednesday rolled around, but Sarah was disappointed when the day passed without the usual walk-through. A department manager told her Kelley was busy making sure the new manager understood the company accounting system she had put into place.

Late Friday afternoon Sarah removed her headset and straightened her desk. She was enjoying her new job, but knew a part of it was due to Kelley Champion's presence. Sarah was looking forward to the weekend off and had promised to take Cherish and Carl to the movie of their choice and then out for burgers or pizza. She was leaving about a half hour later than normal and locked the door to Customer Service behind her. She waved to a few employees she knew as she made her way toward the sliding front doors, waiting as the security guard unlocked them. She fumbled in her purse for her car keys as she thought how wonderful it would be to have the next two days off.

She loved her job, and the weekends allowed her to spend much needed time with her children. Her ex-husband, Clifford, had always lavished attention on Cherish, his little princess. After their divorce, Cliff had suddenly become an absent father, and the ten-year-old missed his undivided attention. Spoiled by him, Cherish blamed Sarah for the divorce and resented the time her mother was away working, a subject the girl never failed to broach at every available opportunity.

As Sarah approached her old, metallic blue Buick Park Avenue, she was surprised to see Kelley leaning against the front of the car. A distinct look of happiness crossed Kelley's face when she saw Sarah coming toward her and she pushed away from the vehicle.

"Need a jump?" Sarah asked, casting a glance at Kelley's familiar white Jeep parked next to her Buick.

"No. I was waiting for you to leave work. I've been a little busy this week and didn't get the chance to pay my weekly visit to Customer Service."

"We missed seeing you," Sarah said, unlocking her driver's side door. "You always make the day pleasant for us."

Kelley slipped her hands into the pockets of her slacks. "I can't promise the new manager will drop by quite as often."

"I heard you might be leaving soon."

"Looks that way. Bilt-Rite will be expanding into the northwest soon and that means new stores to be opened."

"How long will you be gone?"

"I usually travel two months and then come home for two months."

"You travel six months out of the year?"

"Sometimes longer if problems crop up."

"I don't think I could stand being away from home for so long," Sarah said. She tossed her purse into the front seat and closed the car door.

"You have a family. Someone waiting for you to come home each night. Right now I don't have that luxury. But I enjoy the traveling, for the most part."

"No family?"

"I'm an only child and single at the moment. I'll be leaving Monday afternoon, and it may be a little forward of me, but I was hoping you might consider having dinner with me tomorrow evening. Sort of a farewell dinner."

Sarah frowned and looked down at her shoes, regretting her answer. "I'd enjoy that, Ms. Champion. But I promised my kids I'd take them to a movie and out for pizza or hamburgers afterward."

"I understand. It was just a thought. Maybe when I return to Boston," Kelley said with a shrug. "Family is more important. You're doing a great job, by the way. Your first evaluation was very impressive."

"Thank you," Sarah said with a nod. "I know you took a big chance when you hired me, and I wouldn't want to let you down."

"I doubt you'd let me or the company down." Kelley reached around her and opened the car door. A brief scent of Kelley's musky cologne lingered pleasantly in Sarah's nose. "You better get home before it gets any darker. Enjoy your weekend." Kelley backed toward her Jeep and waited as Sarah pulled out of the employee parking lot. Through her rearview mirror Sarah watched Kelley look up at the stars beginning to twinkle in the darkening sky overhead. Sarah had never seen anyone look so alone.

Chapter Two

SARAH DOZED MOST of the flight to Vancouver, her dreams filled with visions of Kelley's smiling face, her gentle, lingering touches. A light shake on her arm woke her. She didn't know how much time had passed.

"We're beginning our descent," Walter whispered.

"Thank you," she answered.

"I've arranged for a car to meet us and take us directly to the hospital."

"Do I look all right?" she asked. "I want to look my best for Kelley."

"You look delicious, my dear."

Sarah felt the emotions she had repressed since they boarded the airplane swell inside her. She didn't know how she would react to seeing her lover of a quarter century lying in a hospital bed, unconscious, unaware, unmoving. She had never seen any weakness in Kelley over the years. Together they'd built a comfortable, prosperous life with Sarah staying at home with the children while Kelley continued to travel half the year opening new stores for the ever-expanding Bilt-Rite Home Centers. Sarah and her children had benefited from Kelley's hard work, and she had denied them nothing, despite the tension between her and Cherish. Sarah glanced across the aisle at Cherish sitting next to Carl. Carl would miss Kelley more than Cherish. Sarah had no doubt about that. She only hoped she and Cherish could manage to get through the next few days in Vancouver without attempting to kill one another.

Sarah leaned back against her seat and turned her head to gaze out the small window as the airplane banked to the right on its approach into Vancouver. When they broke through the overcast skies that seemed to mirror her feelings, the city came into view. It looked larger than she remembered. In the distance, she could see the inlets that connected to the Pacific Ocean.

Five short years earlier, another airplane had brought Sarah and Kelley into Seattle to begin their honeymoon cruise along the Alaskan Inside Passage. Sarah had been as excited as a teenager as she gripped Kelley's hand. The cruise had been a surprise wedding present from Kelley. When her partner of twenty years leaned closer to look out the airplane window at the sunlight sparkling off the tall buildings of the city and the water in the distance; she said,

"I love you, Mrs. Champion."

It was the first time Sarah had been called Mrs. Champion by anyone, and to hear it come huskily from Kelley's throat sent a familiar shiver through her body.

"I've wanted to say that for years," Kelley whispered. "I want you as much today as I did the day we met."

Sarah turned in her seat and stroked Kelley's face. "If you keep saying things like that we'll never see anything on this cruise."

Kelley grasped Sarah's hand and brought it to her lips. "I love you, Sarah, on so many levels I can't count them all. No one deserves to be as happy as you've made me. Thank you for letting me share your life."

Sarah was surprised when she saw the moisture gathering in Kelley's eyes. She never knew what is was, but something in Kelley changed after their wedding. Sarah had always been satisfied with their intimate times together, but during their honeymoon cruise their relationship reached a new level Sarah wouldn't have believed possible.

Their friends often called them the perfect couple. Although their disagreements were few and far between, some had left one of them crying and the other sleeping in the guest bedroom. Now those arguments seemed so silly. Sometimes she thought Kelley deliberately started an argument just so they could make up a few hours later.

Sarah's body jarred slightly as the airplane's wheels touched down on the tarmac and she heard the plane's engines roar as the brakes were activated. Half an hour later Sarah rested against the back seat of the car Walter had waiting for them. There would be no more homecoming celebrations with Kelley. Sarah closed her eyes and let her mind drift into the past again.

Northridge, Massachusetts, Late September, 1984

DURING KELLEY'S FIRST absence after she and Sarah met, she found a reason to call Sarah at least twice a week. She had never met Sarah's children, but always inquired about them. Sarah thought it was sweet, but didn't understand why Kelley would be interested. Their two month separation dragged by for Sarah until the afternoon she received the call that Kelley was home once again.

"Bilt-Rite Customer Service Department, Sarah speaking," she had answered. "How may I help you?"

"Thank God! I had to call three times before I got you," Kelley's voice said cheerfully.

Sarah lowered her voice and tried not to act too excited. "How may I assist you?"

"Probably in a number of ways," Kelley's low voice said. "I was wondering if you would have dinner with me tonight. It's a weekday and won't take away from the time you spend with Cherish and Carl."

"I'm sure we can honor that agreement."

"I'll pick you up after work. I have your address. Is seven too late?"

"How did you get my address?"

"Personnel. My job does have some perks, you know."

"Isn't that an invasion of privacy?"

"Employee relations. I want to make sure all Bilt-Rite employees are treated well."

"Then I'll look forward to it. At seven. What should I wear?"

"Whatever makes you comfortable. Bye."

Sarah wasn't sure why, but was anxious for the remainder of the afternoon to pass by quickly. On her break she arranged for her neighbor's daughter to watch the children. After work, she drove home and prepared dinner for Cherish, Carl, and the babysitter before taking a shower. She didn't know why it seemed so important to dress to please Kelley. She shuffled through her clothes and chose a forest green dress that brought out the color of her eyes and complemented her hair. She was running a brush through her hair and applying her favorite perfume when she heard the doorbell ring. Before she could make her way downstairs, the babysitter opened the door. When Kelley stepped into the foyer, Sarah couldn't believe what an incredibly handsome woman Kelley Champion was. The broad look of happiness that spread across Kelley's face when she saw Sarah coming down the stairs melted Sarah's heart.

"You look lovely, Sarah," Kelley said.

For a reason she didn't understand, Sarah was glad that Kelley found her attractive. She hadn't felt attractive for a long time. She would have loved to throw her arms around Kelley and give her a warm hug to thank her, but it wouldn't be appropriate. "Thank you. So do you," she said instead.

Kelley laughed. "Thanks. I don't think I've ever been called lovely before."

"You're blushing."

"It's probably just the warm weather." Kelley brought her arm from behind her back and presented a small bouquet of flowers to Sarah. "For you. I brought a couple of small presents back for Cherish and Carl as well."

"You didn't have to do that," Sarah said, a pink glow moving up her face.

"Now you're blushing," Kelley laughed.

Carl had been thrilled with the large Bilt-Rite tractor-trailer Kelley gave him. Cherish, however, was less impressed with the soft, pink cashmere sweater, even though it was her favorite color at the time, and only managed to mumble a semi-polite thank you.

A delicious candlelit dinner served at a table for two in a dim, private section of the restaurant seemed like a dream to Sarah. Kelley entertained her with stories about the areas she had scouted for possible future Bilt-Rite Home Centers. Sarah couldn't remember the last time she had laughed so much. Kelley seemed interested in some of the humorous customers Sarah had dealt with as well. After dinner, Kelley ordered two Irish coffees, and they lingered over the remains of their dinner.

When both were sure the magical evening was drawing to a close, Kelley said, "Thank you for having dinner with me, Sarah. This is the first time I've really enjoyed my first evening back."

"It was my pleasure. Which store will you be at while you're home?"

"The main office hasn't decided yet. I get a week off before getting back to the grind."

"Perhaps you'll be assigned to our store. We could use a cheerful face every now and then."

Awkward silence fell over them as they finished their drinks. Finally, Kelley cleared her throat. "This is probably a totally inappropriate way to end a wonderful evening, Sarah, but I want you to know that I like you very much. I can't remember the last time I was this comfortable with anyone."

"Thank you."

"I...uh...don't know how much you know about me, and I want to be completely honest with you."

Sarah stared at her blankly, not understanding what Kelley was saying.

"I just want you to know that I like you...more than a little. I would like to be able to spend more time with you, and your children, of course. I'm not very good with children, but I hope I can figure it out."

"They're not that complicated. You certainly won Carl's undying friendship with the truck."

"I'm sorry I wasn't as successful with your daughter."

"Cherish is at one of those stages where nothing makes her happy. Eventually she'll change and become a completely different girl. Then you'll think you're living out a scene from The Exorcist as her head spins around on her shoulders, and she spits up green pea soup."

"Sounds delightful," Kelley said with a chuckle. "I'd like to see you again, Sarah. Perhaps take you and the children to a movie or something over the weekend."

"They would love that."

"Then it's a date?"

"A date? I suppose it is."

When Kelley escorted Sarah back to her apartment they stood in the hallway chatting amiably as if neither of them wanted the evening to end. Sarah leaned against the apartment door wondering what it would feel like to kiss Kelley goodnight. Then wondered why the hell that thought had popped into her mind. The front door opened unexpectedly, and Sarah nearly fell into her apartment. She reached out and grabbed Kelley's arms and was pulled upright. Standing face-to-face with Kelley, so close the scent of her cologne was intoxicating, Sarah inhaled the essence of Kelley Champion deeply.

"Must have been a really big meal to take this long," Cherish said coldly, staring at her mother in Kelley's arms.

"Next time, give me some warning before you jerk the door open, Cherish," Sarah admonished with a frown. "Why aren't you in bed?"

Kelley released Sarah and awkwardly stuffed her hands into the pockets of her coat. "Well, I'd better be going, Sarah. Call and let me know which movie you decide on and I'll get the tickets before I pick you up."

"What movie?" Cherish asked.

"Ms. Champion is taking all of us to a movie next weekend," Sarah said.

"Which one?"

"Whichever one you decide on," Kelley said.

Cherish thought for a moment and then said, "There's a new horror movie opening next weekend. Mom and Carl and I love horror movies," she said, pointedly staring at Kelley. "Right, Mom?"

"Yes, we do, dear, but Ms. Champion might not be as fond of them as we are."

"I'm fine with that. Just let me know," Kelley shrugged.

SARAH LAY IN the dark of her bedroom and rethought the events of the evening. A date? Well, she hadn't considered going to dinner with Kelley Champion as a date. Not a real date anyway. More like a social engagement. The things Kelley said swirled around her mind. She said she liked Sarah more than a little. She wanted to spend more time with her and the children. She wanted to see Sarah again. Kelley had been a perfect... She threw her arm over her eyes and swallowed hard. She almost thought Kelley had been a perfect "gentleman" all evening. She held doors for Sarah, pulled out her chair, walked her to her door, and had done a dozen other thoughtful things. At the time Sarah thought nothing of them. She liked Kelley. Liked talking to her. But what did she really know about Kelley Champion except that she was a nice person? She was nice to everyone. So why would she be any different toward Sarah?

SARAH NEVER KNEW if it was the movie itself, or spending the afternoon with two young children that had terrified Kelley more. She seemed like such a confident and strong woman. The idea that either would bother her seemed ridiculous. But it was obvious from the moment she picked them up that Kelley Champion was filled with trepidation at the very least. The conversation between them was semi-strained. Watching Kelley trying to lower herself to the children's conversational level was more than a little humorous. Sarah was relieved when Cherish and Carl begged to sit close to the screen, knowing their mother would never sit that close. The two women found seats in the middle of an empty row and settled in with their popcorn and sodas.

Kelley breathed her first relaxed breath when she sat down next to Sarah. They hadn't been in their seats more than a few minutes when the previews for future movies began. Sarah leaned over slightly toward her, their shoulders touching. "Thank you."

"You're welcome, but if I land in your lap because something scares the shit out of me, I hope you'll understand."

"Not a horror fan, huh?"

"I hate them."

"Then why would you agree to this?"

"So I can be with you, of course," Kelley answered, her voice a whisper.

The flickering light from the theater screen partially illuminated Kelley's face, sending her eyes into deep shadows and making it impossible for Sarah to read what might have been in Kelley's eyes. Nearly an hour into the film Kelley's body jumped and her hand flew over her eyes. She was breathing heavier than normal even after she removed her hand and stared down at her lap. Instinctively, Sarah reached out and rested a comforting hand on Kelley's forearm.

"Are you all right?" she asked.

Kelley simply nodded, but refused to look up again. "If I had a bad heart, I'd be dead right now. Sorry."

Sarah slid her hand down Kelley's arm, taking her hand and entwining their fingers. Kelley turned her head, still down. "God, I can't believe I'm such a wuss."

Sarah snickered quietly at the woman next to her. Kelley's temporary loss of cool was worth it if it resulted in holding Kelley's hand. She could spend the remainder of the movie happily absorbing the warmth flowing softly through her body from Kelley's touch. Perhaps if she closed her eyes she would let her imagination take free rein and imagine the heat being generated in other parts of the woman's body. While she was pondering all of the pleasant things that could be, her hand suddenly went cold as Kelley quickly withdrew from hers.

"Wasn't that the coolest thing you've ever seen, Mom?" Carl asked as he climbed into Sarah's lap.

"Very cool," Sarah whispered and kissed the top of his head. Kelley watched as Carl cradled his small body tightly against Sarah's.

"Is he okay?" Kelley asked.

"Yes. But I think that scene a little while ago was probably a little too cool. He just needs some time to get his brave side back."

"Ah, I see," Kelley said with a grin. She leaned closer to Sarah's ear and whispered, "I'm jealous. Can I crawl into your lap the next time I'm scared?"

"Just watch the movie. It'll be over soon."

When the credits began scrolling up the screen, Sarah sent Carl off to find his sister. She stood and stretched. "That boy is heavier than he looks," she remarked.

Kelley picked up their empty drink and popcorn containers and prepared to leave. Sarah had paid very little attention to the movie. Before Carl's interruption she had been distracted by the feel of Kelley's hand in hers and wasn't sure what to make of it. Had she made a mistake, allowing Kelley to overstep the acceptable boundaries of friendship? She was beginning to feel uncomfortable and didn't like or understand the feeling.

"Sarah, I apologize," Kelley said when she saw the look on Sarah's face. "What I said... I should never have said it. It was an inappropriate remark, and I know it made you very uncomfortable. I'll be glad to take you and the kids home if you want. I didn't mean to embarrass you."

"I promised the kids pizza or burgers after the movie. I try not to break my promises to them. They've already been hurt by having too many promises broken," Sarah said with uncharacteristic forcefulness.

"I won't break my promise. I just thought...you know...what I said might have made you too uncomfortable to have dinner. I'll do whatever you think is best."

"I think it would be best to discuss this at a later time," Sarah said when she saw Cherish and Carl walking up the aisle toward them. Kelley shifted uncomfortably from one foot to the other.

PLAYING GAMES WITH Carl at the Pizza Arcade after the movie did manage to relieve some of the stress Kelley was feeling. The 'discussion' Sarah wanted to have made the rest of the afternoon drag by slowly. Cherish and Sarah spent most of their time talking and occasionally playing a more advanced game which was located at the far end of the arcade. Sarah and Kelley had barely exchanged more than two complete sentences in the last two hours. When Sarah announced it was time to go home, Carl cashed in his tickets for a toy that cost less than the games they played to earn the tickets.

Carl latched on to Kelley's hand when she helped him out of the backseat of her car. Sarah unlocked the front door, and took everyone's jackets and hung them in the entry closet.

"I'll get them ready for bed. I'd appreciate it if you'd wait in the living room," Sarah said without looking at Kelley. "There's something I think we need to talk about."

The undeniable feeling of panic caused by her carelessness overwhelmed Kelley as she watched Sarah escort Cherish and Carl up the stairs. It was a cool evening, but her hands were moist with nervous sweat. She balled her hands into fists, hoping to stop the tremble she saw when she looked at them. She had ruined everything because she hadn't been able to keep her mouth shut. *What the hell was I thinking?*

I was thinking how much I want to be with her, she answered herself. I was thinking how beautiful she is. *Why would she want to be with someone like you? She could have her choice of handsome men.* I can give her anything she ever wanted. I'm not poor. I have a nice house. *Yeah, and every time you're out of town you'll be worrying about what she's doing, who she's seeing.* She wouldn't do that! *Everyone you've ever cared about has taken advantage of your good nature. She might be as cute as a bug in a rug, but she is still a woman. She'll have needs and you'll be hundreds of miles away.* No! Sarah's not like that. *That's what you thought with the last woman you thought was THE one and look how that turned out.*

Kelley found a small sheet of stationary on a desk in the living room and dug around carefully in a drawer for something to write with. She quickly penned a short message and folded it in half. *Coward.* Damn right, she told her inner voice as she propped the paper on a small table near the front door and silently left the apartment.

TWO WEEKS PASSED during which time Kelley was assigned to the Northridge store, but she had not gone to the customer service department to see Sarah. After all the flirting Kelley had done, Sarah was becoming more than a little miffed at being ignored. What had she done to make Kelley suddenly distance herself? Even poor little Carl had asked where the truck lady was. When the word came down that Kelley Champion would be leaving again by the end of the week, Sarah knew she had to do something. She would force Kelley to tell her what she had done that made Kelley want to avoid her. She had phoned Kelley's office twice, but her calls had been ignored. As much as she wanted to deny it, Sarah felt an attraction she couldn't identify.

As soon as she was sure the children were asleep, Sarah left her apartment. Fortunately, her neighbor's daughter was free, and Sarah assured her she would probably be gone only a couple of hours. She glanced at the slip of paper in her hand and began driving toward the address. When she pulled to the curb half an hour later, she looked at the buildings lining the street and almost returned home without the confrontation she had planned in her mind for days. Surely the personnel files she had sneaked a peek at were wrong. The older neighborhood was lined with the stately brownstone homes she had drooled over for years. Only the oldest and wealthiest families in the city could afford to live in the Back Bay.

Sarah stepped out of her old Buick and walked down the street, mesmerized by the soft glow of the round, antique-looking streetlights. When she found the number she was searching for, she hesitated before approaching the ornately carved front door. By then her curiosity had kicked into high gear, and she had to see the inside of the home. She stood there going over everything she wanted to ask and say for a few minutes before taking a deep breath and pressing the doorbell. The sound of the chiming from inside the home screamed affluence. She pressed it a second time a minute later, half-hoping Kelley either wasn't home or that this wasn't the correct address. She started to turn away when she heard the sound of the dead bolt opening.

"Sarah," Kelley said with an uncomfortable look on her face. "Is something wrong?"

The sight of Kelley standing in the open doorway dressed in white socks, jeans, and a flannel shirt over a white t-shirt immediately stopped whatever Sarah had planned for her opening volley. Kelley looked adorable, she thought. Then she remembered the purpose of her late evening trip.

"I want to know why you're avoiding me," Sarah said as she stepped past Kelley and entered the brownstone. "I haven't seen or heard from you in two damn weeks."

"I'm not avoiding you," Kelley answered.

"Yes, you are," Sarah said as she turned around, trying her best to look calm. "You were supposed to stay after I put the kids to bed so we could talk."

"That wasn't the message I was getting from the tone of your voice," Kelley said. "I could feel you pushing me away. I figured it was better if I left before we both said things we'd regret."

"Why did you refuse to take my calls?"

"I have a new assignment, and I've been pretty busy getting ready." Kelley stalled.

"You always have a new assignment."

"It's my job. Did you expect me to drop everything just because you called?"

Sarah was momentarily stunned by Kelley's tone and took a step toward her. "I seem to remember that you called me after your last assignment and couldn't wait to see me. What's changed all of a sudden?"

"I made a mistake. You obviously weren't as anxious to see me as I was you. I've already told you I wanted to see you, that I was interested in you and wanted to spend more time with you." Suddenly Kelley couldn't stop talking. Her voice rose and everything she'd been keeping inside boiled over. "What the hell did you think that meant, Sarah? I'm a human being with needs like everyone else. You're a beautiful woman, and I wanted to know you better. A lot better. And I'm not talking about having a sleep-over and gossiping about how far we let our boyfriends go. I sat through that God-awful horror movie and put up with the shitty way that little witch you call a daughter spoke to me and treated me. I put up with all of that because I wanted to be with you, but the tone in your voice that night told me it wasn't going to work out. My friends already think I'm out of my mind because I'm attracted to you. You're not only straight, but you come with a permanent set of baggage. I'd have to be out of my fucking mind to want that kind of drama—"

Sarah silenced Kelley's tirade by covering her lips with her own. How much different could it be to kiss another woman, she thought. She was startled at how soft and supple Kelley's lips were, inviting her to explore as Kelley's arms slipped around her to deepen the kiss.

"Do you know how long I've wanted to kiss you?" Kelley breathed when their lips parted. She brought a hand up between them and touched Sarah's lips with her fingertips. "It was as wonderful as I knew it would be. Thank you."

Sarah didn't know what to say or even why she had kissed

Kelley. She lost herself quickly in Kelley's liquid brown eyes. "You have bedroom eyes," she finally said. Her hand flew to her mouth as if she couldn't believe what she had said.

"You're blushing," Kelley said with a charming smile.

"I'm sure I am," Sarah answered, fanning her face with her hand. "I've never done anything like that before. I don't know what got into me."

"Maybe it was my irresistible charm," Kelley laughed lightly.

"Anything I say will only make it worse."

"Please. Don't be afraid to talk to me. Tell me what you're feeling."

"I...I don't know what I'm feeling. I've never kissed a woman before." Sarah closed her eyes. "I'm scared," she said in a barely audible voice.

"Maybe now is a good time for that 'discussion' you wanted," Kelley suggested.

Kelley took Sarah's hand and led her to the sofa. Sarah sat at one end and Kelley at the other. She brought Sarah's feet up to her lap and began gently massaging them. The look on Sarah's face was blissful.

"So are you going to tell me now why you've been avoiding me like I was Typhoid Mary?" Sarah asked as her whole body began to relax.

"Because you scare the hell out of me, Sarah Turner. You make me feel things I haven't felt before about anyone. You make me say and do things I shouldn't, but when I'm anywhere near you I can't seem to stop myself."

"I'm not a scary person."

"You are to me because I'm very attracted to you, Sarah, and I shouldn't be," Kelley started. "I'm a lesbian and you're not. I don't want either of us to be hurt from the fallout."

"What fallout?"

"Carl and Cherish for one thing. If I did what I wanted to with their mother, how do you think they'd feel? It doesn't take a rocket scientist to figure out that Cherish isn't exactly my number one fan. Hell, I couldn't even bribe her."

"Carl thinks you're wonderful."

"He can be bribed. But will he feel the same way as he gets older and understands what it means that his mother is sleeping with another woman, and not in a sisterly way."

"You might be right," Sarah frowned.

"And then there's you," Kelley said, taking a deep breath.

"What about me?"

"You're straight, Sarah. Most straight women are willing to experiment. You know, see how the other half lives. But it never goes any further than that."

"I'm not experimenting with you," Sarah said.

"I believe you. I can only tell you my feelings. I admit I want to be closer to you," Kelley caught Sarah's eyes. "I will even admit that I want you physically. But I want more than that. Before I get more deeply involved and can't turn back, it's only fair for you to know I want something more permanent, a relationship I can look forward to coming home to every night. I want to share my life with someone. We're not there yet, but if I court you, I'll be damned serious about it."

A pleased look crossed Sarah's face. "I haven't ever been courted."

"After we sat through that terrible movie," Kelley said with a laugh, "and you told me we needed to talk, I was heartbroken. I knew I'd moved too quickly and said too much. I'd blown it and couldn't face you. It was better to simply lick my wounds and skulk away before they got any deeper."

Sarah looked at Kelley and took a deep breath. "I was furious when I drove over here tonight. I've been rehearsing everything I wanted to say to you for days. But now I can't make myself be mad because I know I'm attracted to you too. I don't even know what two women do together, but as curious as I am, I'm not willing to simply fall into bed with you to find out. I like having you in my life, and I've wondered what it would be like to be in your arms a thousand times. At least now I know you're a great kisser," Sarah said.

"I don't get much practice."

"Well, baby, you can practice on me any time you want." Sarah slapped her hand over her eyes to avoid seeing Kelley's smiling face. "Jesus, I can't believe the things you make me think of."

Kelley patted the cushion beside her. "Come here," she said.

Sarah scooted closer and Kelley wrapped an arm around her shoulders. "I'm a huge snuggle fan," she said as she pulled Sarah closer and kissed the top of her head.

"Hmm. I like that, too."

"Then do whatever you're comfortable doing. I would never hurt you. If I do anything that makes you feel uncomfortable, tell me and I'll stop. Be yourself and what happens, happens."

Kelley's fingers softly trailed up and down Sarah's arm. She thought she had died and gone to Heaven when Sarah's arm slipped across her abdomen and gave her a hug. They sat comfortably for several minutes before Sarah looked up at her. Kelley leaned forward slightly and caressed Sarah's cheek. "You're so beautiful," Kelley whispered as she brought their lips together again. She slid her hands beneath Sarah's shirt, her fingers spreading to feel smooth, hot skin. She kneaded the skin as her mouth began moving down Sarah's neck, and her lips felt the heavy beat of blood as she found Sarah's pulse point.

Sarah's hand traveled up Kelley's arm and around her neck. Her lips parted slightly and Kelley answered the invitation to slip her tongue inside. Sarah drew Kelley farther into her mouth and increased the pressure. Desire swept through Sarah, and she felt her body react with a passionate and needy kiss. It had been so long since she had been physically close with anyone, desired by anyone. She shifted her body to straddle Kelley's legs. When the kiss ended, she took Kelley's face in her hands, her breathing labored. Kelley nipped gently at the tender skin below the pulse point and Sarah groaned, holding her more tightly. For a moment she moved to pull away from the mouth that covered and teased the most sensitive spot on her neck, but Kelley, as if knowing the sensitivity she had found, pressed her closer.

"I can't stand it, Kelley," she gasped. "Please. It's too much."

Kelley withdrew from Sarah's neck and waggled her eyebrows. "Too much, huh?"

"The feeling is too intense when you kiss me there."

"What would happen if I didn't stop?"

A blush crept up Sarah's throat. "I'd lose my mind until I was satisfied."

"I'll remember that."

"Do you have a super sensitive spot like that?"

"Of course."

"Where?"

"That's something you'll have to discover."

"No fair."

"But the hunt is so much fun." Kelley leaned back against the couch and took a deep breath. "I was in the middle of fixing dinner when you arrived and now I'm really hungry. Want to join me?"

"What are you having?"

"Tomato soup and a grilled cheese sandwich. I'm never home long enough to stock much food. It just goes bad."

"That sounds like a gourmet meal to me."

Sarah followed Kelley into the kitchen and sat at the small table, watching her reheat the soup and prepare two sandwiches.

"Where are you off to this time?" Sarah asked.

"Olympia, Washington. It looks like most of my work for quite a while will be developing the Pacific Northwest."

"It's a long way from home."

Kelley set a plate and bowl in front of Sarah and poured fresh coffee for her before joining her at the table.

"This coffee will probably keep me up half the night," Sarah said as she brought the cup to her mouth.

"Would you like something else? It doesn't bother me anymore."

"This is fine as long I don't have another cup. Are you from Boston?"

Kelley shook her head as she chewed her first bite. "Vermont."

"It's beautiful there, especially in the fall."

"I inherited this house and our cabin in Vermont when my folks passed away."

"This is a magnificent house. I used to dream about living in one of these old brownstones when I was a kid," Sarah said as she swept her eyes around the spacious kitchen.

"It's too big for only one person though. Most of the rooms haven't been opened for years. My father always complained about how expensive the upkeep on one of these old houses was. I always liked the cabin better, but unfortunately I don't get a chance to go there very often. It needs some renovation work."

"Then you work at the perfect place."

"Yeah. I was thinking maybe over the summer I might take some time off and work on it. Upgrades mostly. My parents and I spent every summer there when I was a kid."

"One of those do-it-yourself types, huh?" Sarah teased.

"A regular power tool fanatic," Kelley laughed. "I'm pretty good with my hands."

"I'll bet you are."

"I...I didn't mean anything by that," Kelley said, red creeping up her neck.

"You're cute when you blush."

Kelley cleared her throat before she could speak again. "Upper level management does not blush," she said with a grin. "We're always calm and cool under pressure."

"Is that a fact?"

"Absolutely."

Sarah picked up her plate and bowl and carried them to the sink. She rinsed the bowl out and leaned against the counter for a moment, her eyes closed in thought. She turned around and watched Kelley shove the last bite of her sandwich into her mouth. She walked back to the table and gathered Kelley's dishes.

"I'll get those," Kelley protested.

"It's okay," Sarah said with a shrug.

The next time she approached the table, she paused next to Kelley for a moment. When Kelley looked up at her, Sarah leaned down and brought her mouth to Kelley's in a tender kiss. Kelley pulled her onto her lap and wrapped her arms around Sarah as the kiss ended.

"It's getting late," Kelley whispered. "I have to get up early and you need to rest so you can do your best on behalf of Bilt-Rite."

"Doesn't keeping you stimulated fall into that category?"

"Personally, I think you deserve a massive raise for making me feel this happy," Kelley beamed.

Sarah leaned closer and smothered Kelley's lips with her own. When the kiss came to an end, she looked at Kelley. "That's a down payment. The sooner you finish your business in Washington, the sooner you can collect the full payment."

Chapter Three

AS THE CAR drew to a stop at the main entrance of St. Paul's Hospital, Sarah stepped from the vehicle filled with the wonderful memories of the new life she'd started with Kelley so long ago. She looked up at the multi-story building, overwhelmed once again with sadness that the life they'd shared would be coming to an end sooner than she wanted.

The door at the entrance of the hospital slid open automatically as Sarah approached it. She hesitated a moment before entering as if her world wouldn't come to an end if she remained outside. A gentle touch to her back by Carl coaxed her forward. Walter stepped to the information counter for directions to the Intensive Care Unit and guided the little group toward the elevators. While they waited for the next elevator, Carl stood beside Sarah and took her hand, squeezing it lightly. She looked up at him and was proud of the man he'd become, gently guided by Kelley's easy-going manner. Kelley had bonded with Carl easily and quickly. Probably their mutual interest in sports, Sarah thought, especially hockey. She remembered the first time her son had come home from practice displaying a bloodied lip. He and Kelley had both been beaming with pride over the injury that appalled Sarah. When Carl gazed down at her now, she could still see a faint hint of that badge of pride above his upper lip.

The Intensive Care Unit was located on the fifth floor. As soon as the elevator doors slid open, Cherish exited and strode immediately to the nursing station. Cherish had grown into a strong and confident young woman. She had also been the source of Kelley's deepest frustration, refusing to accept the relationship between Sarah and "that woman," who had intruded on their lives and seduced her mother.

Cherish met Sarah and the others and said, "They've paged Dr. Gilgannon and want us to meet him in the waiting room."

"You all go on," Sarah said. "I'll join you in a few minutes."

"We can wait for you," Carl said.

"I really need to be alone right now, honey," she said softly. "Just for a few minutes." Sarah waited until Walter and her children entered the waiting room half way down the hall. She walked slowly in the opposite direction and turned the first corner.

CHERISH DROPPED HER purse onto a table under the windows in the family waiting room and took a deep breath. She folded her arms across her chest and stared out the windows at the world below, people moving purposefully, leading their lives as usual. She wondered if they knew the pain and grief that was playing out in the building they walked past. She wished she'd stayed home. If what Walter had told them was confirmed by Kelley's doctor, there was no point in being in Vancouver. Why had she come? To comfort her mother? No matter how hard Cherish tried, she always said something to upset Sarah. She was incapable of not expressing her opinion about Kelley Champion. Even from her death bed, Kelley was doing what she had always done, controlling Sarah.

"Are you all right?" Walter asked as he stood next to Cherish.

"I'm just peachy freakin' keen, Uncle Walter," she answered. "We're all here still jumping through Kelley's hoops."

"You could have stayed in Massachusetts," he said softly.

Cherish looked up at him and shook her head slightly. "I need to be here for Mom. No matter what anyone thinks I love my mother."

"Then try not to say things you know will upset her."

Her mouth lifted in a half smirk. "You know, if there is one thing I did learn from Kelley, it was to speak my mind."

"She made Sarah happy."

"I know that, Uncle Walter. I wish I could have made Mom as happy as Kelley did."

"You were jealous of Kelley?"

"Sounds a little sick doesn't it?" Cherish looked up at Walter. "Does it make me a terrible person?"

"No. It makes you that little girl who missed her father."

Cherish shook her head. "Actually, Kelley was a better parent than my real father."

"Have you ever told her that?"

"And ruin my reputation as the bitch of Boston? Never." She rubbed her arms absently. "The first thing she ever gave me was a beautiful pink cashmere sweater. It was so soft and I loved it. But I refused to let her know that because I knew she was only trying to buy my affection."

Walter and Cherish stood staring out the window for a few minutes. Finally, Cherish broke the silence. "Did Kelley tell you she almost killed me once?" she asked.

Despite his best effort to conceal it, Cherish saw the look of shock on his face. "I didn't think so," she said.

"I'm assuming you weren't injured," Walter finally said.

"Nope." She frowned and gazed into the distance. "Mom

wasn't home. She was off to one of her charity luncheons. She dropped Carl off at a friend's birthday party and left me alone with Kelley."

"How old were you?"

"Thirteen, I think. I don't really remember. Kelley and I started arguing the second Mom left the house. I hated that old barn she lived in. It reminded me of Dark Shadows. You know, that old television show about vampires. That's how I saw Kelley. It seemed like she had sucked the life out of Mom and Carl. Someone had to stand up to her and show Mom the kind of woman she was. At least to a thirteen-year-old." Cherish shook her head and took a deep breath.

"Anyway, apparently she decided I was old enough to start washing my own clothes and take on a few responsibilities around the house to lighten the load on Mom." She laughed humorously. "God! I was such a brat. Kelley was washing up the dishes from breakfast and told me to bring any dishes that might be in my room and Carl's downstairs. I found a couple of pieces of silverware, including a steak knife from the night before. I went back into the kitchen and saw her standing there, her back to me, and I was still pissed. I tossed the knife toward the sink and barely missed her." A short laugh escaped her mouth. "I just realized how psychotic that sounds. Guess I have that to look forward to with Ethan in a few years. Anyway, Kelley turned around and saw me smiling. The next thing I knew she slammed me against a wall and held me there with her wet, soapy hand against my throat, shaking with anger. I'd never seen her that mad before and I never did again."

"Did you ever tell Sarah?"

"No, and I don't think Kelley did either. We never talked about it again. I know she could have hurt me, maybe wanted to, and that scared her a little. I know it scared the hell out of me, but I never told her that."

"Why did you hate her so much?" Walter asked. "It had to be more than teenage rebellion."

"The way I saw it, she took Mom away from me. After Dad left, Mom and Carl were all I had. Kelley won Carl over with all that camping, fishing, and hockey crap, and I lost him too." She took a deep breath. "I was a kid. What the hell did I know? Now she's finally out of our lives. Maybe I wanted to be here so I'd know it was really true."

SARAH STOPPED AT the nurse's station to inquire about the location of the Intensive Care Unit. Before she spoke to anyone she hoped to catch a glimpse of Kelley to prepare herself for what she might see after the doctor told her what she already expected to hear.

She followed the corridor to the next hallway and turned right. The wall to her left was nothing but glass doors and windows. Inside the large, brightly lit room she saw six patients lying on hospital beds, most with what looked like dozens of machines connected to their bodies to assist them with breathing and monitoring every function of their damaged or failing bodies. Sarah wasn't sure she would recognize Kelley beneath all the equipment, but paused to examine each patient struggling to survive. A sign posted on the wall outside each door told her she wouldn't be able to see Kelley for more than fifteen minutes each hour. The six patients were separated from one another by a considerable distance, allowing some space for privacy as well as room for the medical personnel to assist their patients unobstructed. A single chair sat near each bed, but none were occupied. Sarah longed to go inside the room to let Kelley know she wasn't alone anymore. She was there.

As her eyes tracked across the room, Sarah saw a familiar shock of brown hair mixed with streaks of gray and immediately knew it was Kelley. A tube protruded from her tender mouth and tears welled up in Sarah's eyes as she watched Kelley's chest rise and fall in rhythm with the machine attached to the tube. A nurse stood next to the bed and wrote onto a clipboard as she adjusted settings on the machinery. Sarah's hands came up and rested against the cool glass of the hallway window, longing to be closer. The nurse finally stepped away from the bed and turned to speak to someone. A slender, auburn-haired woman wearing comfortable looking slacks and a jacquard pull-over sweater moved closer to the bed. Sarah watched as she took Kelley's hand and gently brushed hair from her forehead. She said something to the nurse before sitting down and drawing the chair closer to the bed. She readjusted the covers and stroked the backs of her fingers up and down Kelley's cheek while she spoke.

Sarah observed the woman interact with Kelley for several minutes until the nurse returned and placed a hand softly on her shoulder. The woman looked up briefly and nodded. She stood and gazed down at Kelley for a moment before leaning over the bed and kissing her forehead. Then she kissed Kelley's hand and placed it back at her side. She took her coat from the back of the chair and slung her shoulder bag over her arm. The nurse escorted the stranger from the room and Sarah listened as they briefly spoke.

"You can visit her again in about an hour, Pauline," the nurse said.

"*Merci.* If I bring a book to read to her, would that be all right?"

"Of course. I'm sure she would enjoy hearing it very much."

"Do you think she knows I'm there?" Sarah saw a tear escape the woman's eye.

"I'm sure she does."

"I will see you in an hour or so then."

"Get something to eat and try to rest a little. We'll contact you if there's any change."

The woman's eyes met Sarah's for an instant as she slipped her coat on and passed her before turning the corner and disappearing. Sarah leaned her forehead against the cool glass and tried to think about what she had seen and heard. Who was the woman with Kelley? She was attractive with dark auburn hair, slightly gray at the temples, and a lightly accented voice. She was about Sarah's height and carried herself with confidence. She was obviously distraught, but Sarah didn't know why. Perhaps she and Kelley worked together and were nothing more than very good friends. Perhaps she was keeping Kelley company until Sarah could arrive. During Sarah's musings a nurse walked out of the ICU and stopped next to her.

"Are you all right?" the nurse asked. "Is there something I can do for you?"

"Who was that woman visiting Kelley Champion?" Sarah asked bluntly.

"That was her wife, Pauline. Why do you ask?"

The nurse's words slammed into Sarah's mind like a body blow, and she nearly doubled over from the pain. She leaned against the glass wall to steady herself, certain her legs wouldn't support her if she attempted to take a step.

The nurse reached out to support Sarah as she slumped against the glass. "Can you make it to that chair?" the nurse asked, motioning across the hall. "Let me call a doctor."

"I'm fine," Sarah managed around the growing lump in her throat. "I just need a minute. Thank you."

Slowly Sarah made her way back toward the waiting room, a thousand questions spinning in her brain.

"Dr. Gilgannon is here, Mom," Carl's voice interrupted her thoughts.

"I need to speak to Walter," she said in response.

"But the doctor.. " Carl started.

"I need to see Walter. Now!" Sarah demanded angrily.

Worry creased Carl's face as he left his mother and rushed back to the waiting room. A moment later, Walter walked calmly out of the room and joined Sarah in the corridor.

"Are you all right, my dear?" he asked. "Carl said you seemed upset."

"Did you know?" she asked pointedly.

A look of incomprehension crossed his face.

"Did you know about...Pauline?" she reiterated.

The change in his expression told Sarah he did.

"Why?" she asked.

"We should hear what Dr. Gilgannon has to say first and then we can talk about Pauline."

Sarah began to shake her head slowly and tears filled her eyes. Walter attempted to gather her in his arms, but anger, mixed with the sense of grief she was already struggling with, overcame the calm façade she had tried so hard to maintain, and she pushed him away. Walter waited until Sarah stopped crying and had regained control of her emotions before following her toward the waiting room.

Dr. Gilgannon stood as Sarah entered the room. He shook her hand and murmured his condolences before they all sat down. Carl patted his mother's hand and cast a concerned look toward her. Cherish sat stiffly in her chair waiting for the doctor to begin.

"As I told Kelley's attorney briefly on the telephone, Mrs. Ch...ma'am, she has suffered a massive stroke. It has left her unable to breathe without assistance and we are monitoring her other vital signs. However, the stroke occurred near the brain stem and there is minimal brain activity at this time. As in any case such as this, there is a very small chance she may regain consciousness," Gilgannon explained.

"But it is unlikely," Sarah said.

"Unfortunately, yes," he said, looking down at his hands. "We will continue to monitor her closely for a day or two." He cleared his throat.

Sarah nodded her understanding. "When can I see her?" she asked softly.

Gilgannon glanced at Walter. "Mr. Blomquist has explained the unusual circumstances to me on the telephone. You may see Kelley whenever you wish, but only for a few minutes." He looked at Carl and Cherish. "You are Mrs. Champion's children?" he asked.

"Yes," Carl answered.

"No," Cherish quickly followed.

Sarah snapped her eyes toward Cherish, but said nothing. Carl started to respond, but the grip of his mother's hand stopped him.

"Well, you may see her one at a time if you wish," Gilgannon said as he stood. "But for no more than fifteen minutes each to give her nurses a chance to continue their care. I wish I could be more optimistic."

"Thank you, Doctor," Walter said, rising to shake Gilgannon's hand.

When the doctor left, Sarah stood and glared at Walter. "I would like to be with my wife now. Then we need to talk, Walter."

Sarah paused at the entrance to the ICU before following a nurse to the side of Kelley's bed. She looked so frail, so helpless. Nothing like the strong, vital woman Sarah had made love to and then kissed goodbye three weeks before. She wanted to scream at Kelley, and ask her why she had felt the need to take a second wife. What had driven her to seek happiness in the arms of another woman? Kelley had been home less than a month before. She seemed happy, and the passion and desire that drove their lovemaking was no less than it had been every time she had come home for the last twenty-five years. Age had slowed them both a little, but Kelley's touch remained as tender and gentle as it always had been. At fifty-seven, Kelley was still a robust lover and Sarah an equally energetic partner. Why had she not noticed a change in their intimacy? Had there been a change and Sarah had been too stupid, too grateful to be loved once again, to see it? As she gazed down at the woman who had been her life, her everything, for a quarter of a century, Sarah felt overwhelmed by her impending loss. She knew Kelley didn't want heroic efforts made to sustain her life if there was no hope of recovery. For a moment, Sarah angrily wanted to punish her in some way for her betrayal. But she loved the woman she looked down upon and had never been able to deny her anything, let alone her final wish.

Sarah pulled the chair closer to the bed and sat down. She took Kelley's hand and brought it to her lips. She examined each of Kelley's fingers. Memories of their life together flooded her mind. God! How much she would miss those deep brown eyes and that stupid lop-sided little grin she saw every time Kelley looked at her. Kelley's eyes always conveyed the want she felt for Sarah, and the grin was her way of telling Sarah she knew her desires would be met when they were alone.

Sarah leaned closer so her mouth was near Kelley's ear. "I'm here, darling," she whispered. "I got here as soon as I could. I miss your touch so much it hurts. I know about Pauline. I don't understand why you needed the touch of another woman, but I know she's as lucky as I am to have been with you."

It seemed as if she had only been in the room a minute when a nurse placed a hand on her shoulder to gently tell her the fifteen minutes were up. She stood, and just as she had seen Pauline do, she rested Kelley's hand on the bed and leaned down to place a lingering kiss on her forehead.

WHEN THEIR CAR dropped them off to check into their hotel, Walter registered them and escorted Sarah to her room. Sarah took her shoes off as Walter lifted her suitcase onto the luggage rack. She excused herself to go into the bathroom while Walter placed an order with room service.

Sarah felt better after she had splashed cold water on her face and changed into more comfortable clothing. They had decided to rest for a few hours before returning to the hospital. The feel of the carpeting beneath her feet made her feel almost normal again as she crossed the room and sat in an armchair near the window and stretched her legs out in front of her.

"Start talking, Walter," she said calmly as she rubbed her temple with her fingertips.

Walter took his suit jacket off and draped it over the back of the chair opposite her. He opened his briefcase and pulled out a small stack of papers as he sat and loosened his necktie.

"These are Kelley's personal papers," he started. "I'm quite sure this is not how she planned for everything to play out, but it was bound to happen at some point." He picked up the top paper. "First the simple part," Walter said with a sigh. "This is a Physician's Directive. I'm sure you know that Kelley didn't wish any extraordinary measures taken to keep her body alive."

"I know that," Sarah said. "One of your associates has the same directive for me in my file."

"I will give this to the doctor when we return to the hospital this evening. It will take the decision-making out of your hands, as well as any guilt you might have later."

"Tell me about Pauline," Sarah said, rubbing her eyes with the heels of her hands.

"I'm incredibly sorry you had to find out about Pauline the way you did. I should have checked to see if she was there."

"Does she know about me?"

"No," Walter said, shaking his head.

"Kelley seems to have put you in a very awkward position."

"She knew I couldn't tell anyone about her personal affairs. That made me the only other person, besides herself, who knew about both you and Pauline." He picked up two more papers. "This is a Canadian marriage certificate dated 2003, the year same sex marriages were made legal in British Columbia. And this is your Massachusetts marriage certificate dated 2004, the year the Commonwealth first allowed marriage between two persons of the same gender."

"So she was already married in Canada when we were married?"

"Yes. Based on what Kelley related to me, and let me know if this is correct, the two of you began living together in 1984 and were married on your twentieth anniversary in 2004."

"That's correct. You and Michael were there."

"Apparently, she began living with Pauline Reynaud in 1994. She didn't tell me much about how they met. She tried to explain it to me, but I never understood her motives. She came to see me to make changes in her will not long before your wedding. I couldn't believe it when she told me she had married Pauline the previous year. I told her she would be a bigamist if she managed to obtain a Massachusetts license. We were all so giddy to finally get the right to marry that I couldn't believe Kelley was willing to make a mockery of it by getting married under false pretenses. It was so unfair to you."

"And what was her explanation? I'd love to hear it."

"That she loved you more than anything in the world. Her life with you was everything she had ever dreamed it could be. Unfortunately, she loved Pauline just as much and didn't want to hurt either of you."

"Obviously she didn't love either of us enough to remain faithful."

"She told me she wouldn't have believed it was possible to love more than one woman at the same time, or to love them both equally, but she did. Other than that, she couldn't explain it herself. She honestly thought she could keep the two lives she'd built separate. I'm sure she never thought she'd die so soon and leave this mess."

"So now what am I supposed to do, Walter? How will I explain this to Carl? He worshipped Kelley. Did she leave a 'directive' to handle that situation, too? Cherish won't give a damn and will probably be delighted to know Kelley wasn't the perfect woman I've always believed she was."

"I don't know how you will explain it to them," Walter said, picking up a thick folded document. "This is Kelley's Last Will and Testament. You are all named in it. How much do you know about Kelley's finances?"

"Not much, but I knew she inherited money from her parents."

"Actually, she is quite a wealthy woman. When her parents passed away they left her with a rather large trust fund. Any money your household needed came from her work. Any money Pauline needed came from a bank account set up in both their names which was funded by her trust. The money in the trust will be divided equally between you and Pauline, minus the provisions she made for Carl, Cherish, and Ethan. You get the titles to the cabin and the brownstone. Pauline will get the title to the building which houses her bookstore and the living area above it."

"Pauline has no children?"

"No."

"When will you speak to her?"

"Soon. Kelley also left a directive for her cremation."

"I knew that was her preference." Sarah laughed without humor. "My God! Listen to me. I'm talking as if Kelley is already dead."

"As cruel as this may sound, Sarah, for all intents and purposes, she is. I'm so sorry for your loss. I'm losing a close friend as well."

A knock at the door announced the arrival of the order from room service. Once a carafe of coffee and two club sandwiches were set in front of them, the room fell silent. Sarah had no appetite, but knew she had to eat and forced the food into her mouth.

"I'm well aware of attorney-client privilege, Walter, but after Kelley...dies, that privilege should be irrelevant. Please tell me I won't be facing the prospect of other Mrs. Champions."

"There was no one else who shared Kelley's life other than you and Pauline," Walter answered with an attempt at a smile.

"How do you think this Pauline will take all of this?" she asked as she washed her food down with a swallow of coffee.

"I have no idea. I'm sure she will be as upset as you are."

Chapter Four

PAULINE CHAMPION LEFT St. Paul's Hospital and made her way through the large parking lot toward her car. She would be able to see Kelley again in about an hour, but needed to make sure there were no problems at her bookstore before she returned. She sat in her car a few minutes, staring at nothing through the windshield. It had been two days since Kelley collapsed in the living room of their apartment. Pauline remembered all too well her panic when Kelley didn't respond to her name as she called it again and again while she waited for the ambulance to arrive. Kelley had always been so strong, so healthy, so alive. To see her attached to machinery now tore Pauline's heart to pieces. When she contacted Kelley's attorney in Boston, he had asked that Kelley be kept alive until his arrival for some reason. Dr. Gilgannon had offered her little hope, and Pauline desperately needed Kelley to take her in her arms and tell her everything would be all right. As independent as Pauline liked to think of herself, she knew her life would be empty without Kelley. She lowered her head and rested it on her hands as she gripped the steering wheel tightly. At last, she allowed the tears to flow freely, her wracking sobs unheard outside the car.

When she felt calm enough to drive, Pauline turned the key in the ignition and shifted into drive. She paused to judge the speed of on-coming traffic and pulled away from the hospital. Halfway home, she looked at the buildings she passed and saw the Bilt-Rite Home Center where she first met Kelley Champion almost sixteen years before.

Vancouver, British Columbia, April, 1994

PAULINE REYNAUD STRODE into the newly opened Bilt-Rite Home Center and glanced around. She didn't have much time, but wanted to look for materials which could be used to build a new counter space for her small independent bookstore. Business had been slow when the store first opened the previous year, but thanks to a revitalization program, shoppers were beginning to come into the area in greater numbers. As a result, she had recently been able to hire a new clerk, which gave her a little extra time to devote to customer service and the ever-present bookkeeping chores.

She wandered up and down the aisles looking at materials

without really knowing what she wanted. She would need to hire a carpenter to do the actual work, but didn't want to overspend on materials. She stopped in front of a flooring display and stood with a hand on her left hip, attempting to mentally estimate the cost of a particular piece of ceramic tile. She ran a hand through her dark hair and expelled a frustrated breath.

"You look a little lost. Is there something I can help you with?" someone asked.

Pauline turned her head and found the source of the question. A pleasant, but somewhat ordinary looking woman who appeared to be about her age stood nearby, with a crooked smile on her lips.

"I don't know. Everything in here is so confusing," Pauline answered.

"Are you planning a project? Perhaps if you tell me what you have in mind I can suggest something."

"I am hoping to have a new counter built in my store."

"What kind of store is it?" the woman asked as she moved closer. She extended her hand. "My name is Kelley, and I'll be glad to help you."

"I own a bookstore near the downtown area."

"Is that in the area the city recently refurbished to bring in more customers?"

"Yes," Pauline said. "You know the area?"

"I've driven by there, but haven't had time to do much shopping."

Pauline eagerly pulled a business card from her pocket and handed it to Kelley. "Please come by. Are you a reader?"

"When I have the time. Perhaps we can kill two birds with one stone," Kelley said, tapping the business card against her fingertips. "How about I come in and purchase a book this evening or tomorrow? It would give me a chance to look at the area inside the store where you wish to place a new counter. Unless you have something specific already in mind, of course. I could suggest all kinds of things right now, but without seeing the space and the current décor inside the store, it would just be a shot in the dark and probably a waste of your money."

Pauline raised her eyebrows in surprise. "That would be wonderful, and I'd appreciate it very much." She leaned a little closer to Kelley and lowered her voice while resting a hand on Kelley's arm. "Quite honestly, I don't know one end of a hammer from the other, so I would welcome whatever assistance I can get. It's only a small counter and probably won't matter to my customers."

"But it matters to you," Kelley said. "And that's what should matter. If we can't make our customers happy then we've failed to do our job."

Pauline extended her hand. "It was a pleasure to meet you, Kelley. Is this your department?"

"No. I kind of float around from place to place trying to make our customers happy. It was nice to meet you, too, Ms. Reynaud," Kelley said, looking at the name on the business card.

"It's pronounced Ray- no," Pauline corrected.

"I thought I noticed an accent."

"I moved here from Quebec a few years ago, but my English is improving."

"Your accent is delightful," Kelley said just before she was distracted by a store employee tapping her on the shoulder and whispering something into her ear. "We seem to have a minor emergency in plumbing," Kelley explained as she turned to leave. "I'll see you soon, Ms. Reynaud," Kelley laughed over her shoulder as she pronounced Pauline's last name with an accent that would have made Maurice Chevalier proud.

Pauline waved as she watched Kelley trot away. Probably never see her again, she thought. But she was attractive in a friendly, understated sort of way.

PAULINE WAS PULLED abruptly from her thoughts by a horn behind her blaring. She turned off the main road and drove down a few blocks to her store. When she entered the bookstore, she inhaled deeply. She loved the smell of books and their scent gave her renewed energy.

"How is Kelley?" Suzanne, her clerk, asked. "Has she awakened yet?"

"No. Not yet," Pauline answered. Not ever, she thought. "Have there been any calamities while I was gone?"

"Nothing I couldn't handle. Is there a book shipment coming in today?"

"Tomorrow. I will be here to accept it."

"You need to be at the hospital with Kelley. I'll sign for the new books and inventory them for you between customers."

"I appreciate that, Suzanne."

"It's not the same without seeing her here when she's in town."

"I know," Pauline barely managed before her throat threatened to close around the lump growing inside it. "I'm going upstairs to rest for a while. Please call me if you need my assistance."

"I got it covered, boss," Suzanne assured her.

Pauline trudged up the stairs and unlocked her apartment. When she stepped inside, the quiet was overwhelming. Kelley wasn't there puttering around, preparing dinner. She wasn't there to take Pauline into her arms, leaving her senseless after a welcoming kiss. Pauline wandered into their bedroom and leaned against the door frame. Kelley's job, shuttling back and forth between Vancouver and the company headquarters in Boston, meant Pauline only saw her for two months at a time. Even then, as Kelley oversaw stores throughout the northwest, she would often be gone for two or three days visiting stores before returning to their home. Now she felt she had been robbed of their precious time together. How could she sleep again without Kelley's arm around her or without that last kiss to the back of her neck before she fell asleep. She covered her eyes with her hands and choked back her grief. She removed her shoes and crawled across their bed to Kelley's side. She wrapped her arms around Kelley's pillow and buried her face in it, inhaling the scent of her lover before fading off to sleep and her memories.

Vancouver, British Columbia, April, 1994

TWO DAYS AFTER Pauline's visit to the Bilt-Rite Home Center and half an hour before closing time at her book store, Pauline sat behind her desk in the back room struggling with the numbers on her accounting system. Whoever designed this method must have been an expert in hieroglyphics, she thought. Who could possibly understand this?

"A customer is asking for you, Pauline," her clerk said as she poked her head into the office.

"In a moment," Pauline said absently. A few minutes later she threw her hands up and stood, taking a moment to smooth down her slacks and blouse to make herself more presentable. She looked around, but didn't see anyone. She caught movement from the corner of her eye and saw her clerk pointing toward the back of the store. Pauline pasted a welcoming look on her face and moved down an aisle, stopping once to straighten the books on a shelf. She walked to the end of the aisle and turned sharply, looking for the customer. Just as she made the turn she collided with another woman.

"Oh, I am so sorry," Pauline said. When she looked up she recognized the woman from the new home improvement center.

"If you scurry around like that all the time, you may want to consider one of those beeping lights we have to warn our customers about forklifts," Kelley warned playfully.

Trying to look offended, Pauline retorted, "I beg your pardon, but I do not 'scurry.'" Unable to hold her offended look very long, Pauline started to laugh. "Did you find a book you might be interested in?" she asked when she collected herself.

"I enjoy a good mystery when I can find one," Kelley said, holding up a book. "Would you recommend this one?"

Pauline took the book and looked at it. "Yes, this one you should like very much."

"Have you read it?"

"Yes, I have. The author is one of my favorites."

"I'll take your word for it," Kelley said with a lop-sided grin.

As they walked toward the front counter Pauline said, "You'll have to let me know whether you enjoy it or not. One person's taste is often different from another's."

Kelley took out her wallet and placed a credit card on the counter for the clerk. Pauline glanced down at it. It was a corporate credit card.

"Do you need to see my identification?" Kelley asked.

"No. This is fine. Do all Bilt-Rite employees have a company credit card?"

"No, and I never did properly introduce myself." Kelley held her hand out. "I'm Kelley Champion, the interim manger of the new Bilt-Rite Home Center. The permanent manager will be on-site in a couple of weeks."

"Does that mean you'll be leaving then?" Pauline asked.

"For a while, but I'll be back a few times to make sure everything is running smoothly."

"I hope you'll come by when you're in town. To purchase another book."

Kelley cleared her throat and asked, "Is this the counter you want to replace?"

"Yes," Pauline answered, glad that the conversation was turning to something more business-like.

"What did you have in mind exactly?" Kelley asked as she signed the credit slip and took her package from the clerk.

"We'll be closing in a few minutes and there really isn't time..."

"If you haven't eaten already perhaps you will join me for dinner and we can discuss it," Kelley said. She looked around the store before speaking again. "Your décor is simple, yet modern. I think you should stay with that theme and be able to create a simple, but utilitarian counter space with plenty of storage underneath. You need the displays you have on the counter, but may be able to install a wider counter so your check-out area won't be overcrowded."

In a tacit acceptance of the invitation, Pauline said, "We can discuss it more over dinner." Pauline shook her head slightly as she began the process of closing out the cash register for the evening.

What was it about this interesting woman that attracted her? Kelley Champion had done nothing flirtatious, but the way she moved and looked sent tremors through Pauline's body. And, if her choice of reading material was any indication, and it usually was, Kelley Champion was also a lesbian. No, Pauline thought, she is nothing more than a nice lady working overtime to please a customer and bring business to her new store. Pauline blushed at her own thoughts as she considered all the ways Kelley Champion might be able to please her.

Over dinner at a quiet little café not far from the bookstore, Pauline and Kelley discussed what type of counter would be best. Kelley used up a number of napkins, making drawings of the dimensions and space available. Kelley estimated it would take three or four days for the counter to be assembled.

"If you're not in a huge hurry, I would be glad to come by the store after work or perhaps over the weekend and build the cabinet for you," Kelley volunteered. "I'm not an expert carpenter, but do have some experience."

"Ah, one of those power tool women," Pauline laughed.

Kelley cut a piece of steak and nodded as she put it in her mouth. "Anything for a customer."

"And how much might such a project cost, including labor?"

"I get a pretty healthy discount on materials," Kelley said. "And maybe we can take the cost of labor out in kind."

"In kind?"

"You know, trade one thing for another. It's a very old American concept, the ever popular barter system. I give you something you want and you give me something I want in return."

"And what is it you would want, Kelley Champion?"

Kelley's eyes met Pauline's for an instant. "Books, of course," she said. "What else?"

By the following Saturday, the new counter was built and anchored in place. All that remained to be done was staining the wood to match the other décor within the store. Pauline chose a dark cherry finish to match her bookshelves. As soon as the store closed that evening, Kelley began applying stain to the sanded wood. A couple of hours later, she pushed herself off the floor and wiped her cherry-stained hands with a cloth.

"I'm not the neatest stain applier on the planet, but managed not to get it on anything else," she said.

"It looks beautiful," Pauline said.

"One more coat tomorrow should finish it off. This is a pretty quick drying stain, exclusive to Bilt-Rite."

"Then your work here will be done," Pauline said.

"Pretty much," Kelley agreed.

"Can I offer you a glass of wine for a job well done?"

"Sure, why not?" Kelley said after a minute's thought. "I don't have to go in to work tomorrow."

Kelley followed Pauline up the stairs to her second floor apartment. She washed and dried her hands to remove the last of the stain and wandered over to a window overlooking the street. She took the glass of wine Pauline brought to her and said, "They've really done a great job bringing life back to this area."

"It's beautiful at night with the new lights hanging along the streets. I can see them from my bed at night and they almost transport me back to an earlier time when life was not so complicated."

"Is your life complicated, Pauline?" Kelley asked.

"It once was, but not any longer." Pauline gazed into the glass in her hands for a moment before taking another drink.

"Did she hurt you badly?"

Pauline turned her head to look at Kelley. "Yes, but as you can see, I survived. That is how a little Quebecois girl came to live in Vancouver, a continent away from home. I followed my heart without knowing it had never been accepted."

"But now you're wiser."

"And older," Pauline laughed.

"You're beautiful. Any man, or woman, would be lucky to be with you. Whoever it was, was a fool."

"You do not know me, Kelley. Not really. I can be extremely difficult at times."

Kelley set her glass on a table beneath the window and did the same with Pauline's. She stepped closer to Pauline and took her face in her hands. "Difficult or not, you are still a beautiful woman," she said.

"Kelley..."

"Tell me to stop and I will," Kelley said as she softly kissed Pauline's cheeks.

"Don't...stop," Pauline breathed as their lips met for the first time. It had been a long time since Pauline had been kissed by someone who mattered to her. She wrapped her arms around Kelley's neck and gave back every ounce of passion she had through that kiss.

When Pauline rolled over the next morning her body felt alive for the first time in more years than she wanted to think about. A groan of satisfaction lazily escaped her lips as she stretched and inhaled the scent of her lovemaking with Kelley the night before. The thought of a repeat performance shattered when she opened her eyes to find her bed empty. She fell onto her back and threw her arm over her eyes. She was alone. Had Kelley used her and then abandoned her with nothing more than the memory of an incredible night of passion? Even though her brain had been overcome with the desire and attention Kelley lavished upon her, she would have sworn Kelley told her she loved her. Or was that nothing more than the fantasy of a lonely, starving woman?

The sound of the doorknob jiggling and someone entering the apartment startled her. She got out of bed and quietly slipped on her robe. The sound of footsteps roaming through her apartment, going through drawers and cabinets gave her a moment of panic. She picked up the baseball bat she kept behind her chest of drawers and tip-toed to the partially closed bedroom door. Before she could act, the footsteps were coming toward her and she pressed her body against the wall behind the door and raised the bat to defend herself.

"Get up, woman," Kelley said. "I have plans for you today."

Pauline dropped the bat, and her hands flew to her face. Kelley spun around, her eyes widening when she saw the bat at her feet. She swallowed audibly as she held out a plate of Danish and a cup of coffee toward Pauline. "I'm starving after last night, aren't you?"

Pauline stepped into Kelley's arms and hugged her tightly, nearly causing her to drop the plate and cup. She peppered Kelley's face with kisses as Kelley tried to speak. After the final crushing kiss Kelley said, with a waggle of her eyebrows, "You know, sweetheart, I could do so much more if my hands weren't full."

"I could have killed you!" Pauline exclaimed. "You scared the shit out of me. When I woke up you weren't here. I thought you'd left me alone after you got what you wanted last night. I didn't know what to think. Did you take my keys? What were you..."

Kelley set the plate and cup down and shut Pauline up the only way she could think of. She jerked Pauline toward her and covered her mouth with her own. She was greeted with feeble resistance and stroked Pauline's hair as they both settled into a comfortable and probing kiss. When Kelley brought the kiss to an end, she held Pauline.

"Yes, love," Kelley said softly. "I borrowed your keys to leave and get breakfast. I'm not really much of a cook and didn't see anything in the refrigerator. I thought I'd be back before you woke up." She stepped away from Pauline a little and grasped her by the upper arms. "Did you really think I would sleep with you and then simply leave you the next morning? Sneak out like a coward and abandon you? I would never – never – do that to you. Do you believe me?"

"I...I believe you. I'm sorry," Pauline muttered without meeting Kelley's eyes. "Please don't be angry with me."

"I'm not mad at you, baby. Please, look at me." Kelley brought a hand up to caress Pauline's cheek and saw the short, involuntary flinch. She caressed Pauline's face gently and let her fingers slip down to under her chin. With very little pressure she lifted Pauline's chin until their eyes met. "Is that what happened with the fool you were with when you came to Vancouver?" Kelley asked softly.

"It wasn't her fault. She was under so much stress, and I did things deliberately that made her angry," Pauline babbled.

"That's bullshit, honey. You should have had her arrested."

Pauline stepped away from Kelley and went to the window. She pulled the sheer curtain aside and looked out. "I was going to, but while I was in the emergency room her friends convinced me not to. It would look bad for the lesbian community if anyone found out about it, so I didn't." Pauline wrapped her arms around herself and took a deep breath.

Kelley came up behind her and pulled Pauline back against her. "Were you badly hurt?"

"A broken arm and a broken nose, both of which healed with time. I—I think she had sex with me while I was unconscious," Pauline said, shaking her head. "I know she did. She raped me." Tears filled Pauline's eyes as she turned in Kelley's arms to be held. "I haven't been with anyone I cared about since then, until last night."

"Where is she now?"

"Some friends bought her a ticket and she flew back to Quebec the next day. I don't know where she is now."

Still looking into Pauline's blue eyes, Kelley made sure she had Pauline's undivided attention. "You don't ever have to be afraid of me, Pauline. I love you and won't hurt you. If I do, please pick up that baseball bat and smack me with it."

When Pauline laughed a little and sniffed, Kelley said, "Now, how about some breakfast? I'll reheat the coffee. Climb back in bed and I'll bring it to you." Over her shoulder as she left the room, Kelley added, "Then I plan to ravish that magnificent body again!"

Chapter Five

PAULINE RUBBED HER forehead with her thumb and middle finger and shook her head slightly as she gazed out her bedroom window. It had taken her months to adjust to Kelley's work and travel schedule, but eventually she knew Kelley's return was something special to look forward to. Pauline planned her own schedule to spend a few days welcoming Kelley home. Kelley called her every day while she was away and never forgot to say "I love you" and "I miss you." Now Pauline would never hear those words from Kelley again. The years she'd spent with Kelley had been the happiest of her life, and now her lover's life had been cut short without warning.

She looked at her wristwatch. She had called Kelley's attorney in Boston the day of Kelley's collapse, and he promised to fly to Vancouver as soon as possible. He had asked Pauline to allow Kelley to be placed on whatever life support she needed until he could get there. The phone call announcing his arrival had come the previous night. He asked her to meet him in one of the hospital conference rooms the next day, later in the afternoon. Although Pauline, as Kelley's wife, knew her wishes, Walter had her Physician's Directive, and would present it to the doctor to avoid any legal complications that might arise.

SARAH PACED BACK and forth in the hospital conference room on the same floor as the Intensive Care Unit. She stopped in front of the large window overlooking the park-like grounds in the rear of the hospital for a few moments and then resumed her pacing. She was dressed comfortably in an outfit Kelley said made Sarah's eyes stand out. The dark green jacket over a white shell and tan slacks was warm enough for the early fall temperatures, yet not too heavy. Sarah's blonde hair swept loosely around her face.

"Will you please sit down," Walter said. "Pacing doesn't make the time go by any faster."

"I need to see Kelley," Sarah said. "She'll wonder where the hell I am. I promised to come back."

"She'll forgive you, Sarah. She knew we'd have to go through this eventually."

"But not this soon. Kelley's only fifty-seven. Our doctor in Boston did a complete physical on her not six months ago and said she was in perfect health. I should sue that quack."

"Something like this obviously was totally unforeseen. No one could have known or predicted it would happen."

"You mean like me not knowing she had another wife?" Sarah said in a raised voice. "If she weren't already in a coma, I'd put her in one."

"If you don't calm down, I'll have to ask you to leave, Sarah. This is a difficult enough situation without hysterics becoming involved."

"You wouldn't dare!" Sarah seethed.

"Kelley was my friend and client. I promised her I would take care of everything when the time came. And now it has. She's gone, Sarah. As much as we both hate it, it's the truth. The sooner this is taken care of, the better off we'll all be. If you insist on being here, you'll have to sit down and shut up."

"But..."

"Not one peep. Understand?"

Sarah took a chair near Walter and sat down, pouting at being treated like a recalcitrant child and embarrassed by her behavior.

"What do you know about this woman, Walter? Is she some kind of gold digger who took advantage of Kelley for her money? Feel free to say yes to that question," Sarah fumed.

"I've never met her and have only spoken to her twice. Both were limited conversations, and I didn't have a chance to ask about her gold digger status," Walter answered.

A light knock at the conference room door made Sarah sit up and straighten her shoulders in an attempt to look composed and dignified. She took a deep breath and released it slowly as Walter gave her a warning look and crossed the room to open the door."

Sarah watched the woman who had been with Kelley the day before step into the room and extend a hand toward Walter. Once again she was casually dressed and Sarah couldn't help but notice the athletic way in which she carried herself. "*Monsieur* Blomquist?" Pauline asked.

"Yes, Mrs. Champion. I'm so sorry we have to meet under these circumstances. Please take a seat, and I'll make this as quick and painless as I can."

Sarah flinched at hearing Walter address the woman as Mrs. Champion and balled her hands into fists in her lap. As she watched the interloper into her life take a seat across from her, the bluest eyes she had ever seen looked back at her from beneath wispy auburn bangs. The woman's eyes reminded Sarah of the blue-tinted glaciers she and Kelley seen during their Alaskan honeymoon cruise a few years earlier.

Pauline adjusted herself in the chair across from Walter and nodded in Sarah's direction, managing to move the corners of her lips upward a little. Sarah wondered what Pauline's reaction would be to the bombshell Walter was about to drop on her. Like a nuclear weapon, the fallout could be devastating to them all.

As he always did, Walter cleared his throat and took a drink of water from a nearby glass before beginning. "First of all, Mrs. Champion, I want to thank you for honoring my request that Kelley be kept alive until I arrived. You'll understand why that was so important in a moment."

Walter removed the same papers he had shown Sarah the evening before from his briefcase and spread them out on the conference table. "This is the Physician's Directive I spoke to you about, and I'll present it to Dr. Gilgannon after this meeting."

"This will allow the machines to be turned off?" Pauline asked.

"That's correct and even though you are Kelley's legal spouse in Canada, you cannot supercede this document."

"I understand."

Walter picked up what Sarah already knew were the two marriage licenses and closed her eyes. "This is a copy of your marriage license here in British Columbia."

Pauline's eyes softened, obviously from personal memories triggered by the document. Sarah could barely restrain herself from reaching across the table and slapping the pleasant look from Pauline Champion's face.

"And this," Walter said as he held up the other document, "is the marriage license issued to Kelley Champion and Sarah Turner in 2004 by the Commonwealth of Massachusetts in the United States."

A confused look crossed Pauline's face. "You are telling me Kelley had been married before?"

"No, I'm telling you that Kelley was married to you as well as this lady seated next to me. Pauline Reynaud Champion, this is Sarah Turner Champion. You are both the wives of Kelley Barrett Champion."

"But we have lived together for nearly sixteen years!" Pauline protested with a flash of anger directed toward Sarah.

"And *we* lived together for twenty-five years," Sarah spat back.

"But how is this possible?" Pauline asked, looking back and forth from Walter to Sarah.

"I'll try to explain as simply as I can, Mrs. Champion," Walter said.

"Why don't you call us by our first names, for God's sake, Walter? It's just too damned confusing otherwise," Sarah said, her eyes riveted on the woman across the table.

"Fine," Walter said. "Kelley married you, Pauline, in 2003

when same sex marriages became legal in British Columbia. Is that correct?"

"Yes."

"And I believe the Canadian paperwork asked whether you currently were or ever had been married."

Pauline's eyebrows knitted together and she nodded.

"At the time of your marriage to Kelley she was not yet legally married to Sarah although they had lived together for nearly twenty years. When same gender marriages became legal in Massachusetts the following year, Kelley and Sarah were married. Apparently, Kelley lied about whether or not she was already married on the Massachusetts marriage application. Evidence of her marriage to you the previous year was not found, for whatever reason, and the license was granted and they were married."

"So our marriage was legal?" Pauline asked.

"That's correct."

"And Kelley's marriage to this woman?"

"Was not legal." Walter turned to face Sarah. "I'm so sorry, Sarah. Technically and legally, Kelley was a bigamist."

"Why didn't you tell me that last night?" Sarah asked, glaring at Walter.

"Because it wouldn't have changed anything. Kelley obviously cannot be prosecuted and her Will clearly divides her property equally between you."

"What does this mean?" Pauline asked.

Pauline looked across the table at Sarah. It was obvious from what Sarah saw in her eyes that Pauline was hurt and more than a little angered by what she almost certainly considered Kelley's betrayal. Pauline was an attractive woman with beautiful blue eyes and Sarah, much to her chagrin, had no difficulty believing Kelley would have been attracted to her.

Walter waited for a moment hoping the tension in the room would lessen. "Quite a bit will depend on you, specifically whether you wish to fight the provisions of Kelley's Will."

"I am not interested in profiting from my wife's death," Pauline said. "Kelley is a fair woman, and I trust her judgment."

"That answers the gold digger question," Sarah mumbled under her breath. Under the table Walter's hand squeezed Sarah's leg in warning.

"Did Kelley tell you her wishes should anything happen to her?" Walter asked.

"I know she would hate what is happening to her as we speak."

"And you will not oppose the Physician's Directive that she be disconnected from the machinery?"

"Of course not. I will honor my wife's wishes." She glanced at Sarah. "Do you oppose Kelley's request?"

"No. She wouldn't want this and neither would I. As Walter has recently reminded me, Kelley is already...gone," Sarah said, her voice cracking.

"When will this happen?" Pauline asked quietly.

"This evening," Walter replied.

"The children will be here in about an hour to say their final goodbyes," Sarah said.

"You and Kelley have children?" Pauline gasped.

"Two. They are mine from a previous marriage, but Kelley cared for them as if they were her own."

"She was a very giving and loving woman," Pauline stated, almost as if to console Sarah.

"Kelley has already made arrangements for her cremation with a local funeral home here in Vancouver and had the same arrangement with a company in Boston, should she pass away there," Walter said.

"Well, she seems to have thought of just about every damn little thing, hasn't she?" Sarah snorted. "Everything except how we might feel about what she's done."

"Sarah," Walter said, his voice carrying a warning. "Once the doctor pronounces Kelley dead we will return here, and I will read the contents of her Will. Then we can all go our separate ways. Do either of you have any questions?" Walter paused for a moment and then stood. "I'll locate Dr. Gilgannon," he said.

Sarah and Pauline sat in silence, both trying to absorb and come to grips with what was happening. Both had known Kelley in the most intimate way possible between two human beings, and yet they had not known her deepest secret. Sarah closed her eyes and leaned her head against the back of her chair, wishing it was all over with and she could return home. But what would she return to except solitude and perhaps pity from her friends over her loss. Would she ever be able to tell anyone about the other Mrs. Champion? Obviously, no one knew and she decided never to tell anyone. Pauline was another life, a different life, from the one she had shared with Kelley for so many years. There was no reason for anyone to know.

"Can you...can you tell me what happened the day Kelley...when she... Had she been ill? She sounded fine when I spoke to her earlier that day."

Pauline rubbed her temple and closed her eyes before speaking. "She was not ill to my knowledge. The day before she mentioned a headache, but it passed after we ate dinner. I didn't think anything of it, and I'm sure Kelley didn't either. It's not uncommon to have a mild headache when one is hungry. We went to bed early that night. Kelley had to drive into Washington before daylight the next morning. I spoke to her at noon as usual when she took her lunch break and she seemed fine, laughing and teasing as she always did.

"She returned home a little earlier than usual. She seemed the same. Greeted me as warmly as always and inquired about dinner. I suggested she take a shower and change while I finished preparing a salad." Pauline stopped and squeezed her eyes closed. "She said something to me, but I didn't understand her and asked her to repeat it. She did, but it seemed to be random words that made no sense. Kelley must have seen my confusion and tried once again. I started to say something...I can't remember what it was now..., but I saw something in her eyes. Confusion? Fear? I don't know. She turned away, as if to walk to our bedroom and change clothes. Two steps later she collapsed to the floor. She didn't make any attempt to break her fall." Pauline looked down and Sarah saw tears drop from her eyes. "Her head...hit the floor with a sickening sound. I rushed to her and rolled her over, but she couldn't speak. Her eyes stared up at me and moved around. It was as if she didn't see me. I reached for the phone and contacted emergency services. Then I sat with her on the floor, her head in my lap, until the paramedics arrived."

Pauline poured a tumbler of water. Her hand shook slightly, and she drank as if she were parched. She wiped her eyes and tried to compose herself. "When we arrived at the emergency room she was taken back immediately. I waited, half out of my mind with worry, for nearly two hours before Dr. Gilgannon found me and told me Kelley's condition. She was having trouble breathing, but the doctor said she was holding her own and had been placed on a ventilator to assist her. I was relieved, of course, and hoped whatever it was would pass. I sat with her perhaps less than an hour. Suddenly...suddenly the machines monitoring her went berserk. Bells rang and lights flashed as her body stiffened and began to jerk from a seizure. Doctors and nurses poured into the room and I watched from the far corner as they worked to stop the seizure, but it seemed to go on forever. They did everything they could. Finally her body went limp on the bed. She stopped breathing and there was no heartbeat." Pauline seemed to be reliving the terrifying moments she had witnessed. "When her heart began to beat again, Dr. Gilgannon examined her and then escorted me out of the room. That's when he told me her — her brain was no longer active."

Sarah felt suddenly ashamed of the terrible things she had thought about Pauline Champion. Even though Sarah could barely force herself to think about Kelley with another woman, she was glad Kelley hadn't been alone when the stroke hit her. It wasn't Sarah, but she had been with someone who cared about her and obviously loved her. She wasn't sure she would have held up quite as well.

SARAH OPENED HER eyes when the conference room door opened again. She put on a brave face as she rose to greet Carl and Cherish who were accompanied by Walter. She hugged them both and held back her tears. She saw Cherish looking at Pauline and turned around to make the introductions.

"Carl, Cherish, this is Pauline Champion," Sarah announced clearly.

Carl went to the other woman in the room and shook her hand. "Are you Kelley's sister?" he asked.

"No," Sarah said. "She is Kelley's — wife."

"What?" Cherish said loudly. "But you're Kelley's wife, at least in Massachusetts."

"We are both Kelley's wives, it seems," Sarah said, her voice short. She looked at Pauline and Walter. "I'm sorry, but could you both excuse us for a minute? I need to speak to my children alone."

"Certainly," Pauline nodded as Cherish's eyes hurled daggers at her.

When Pauline closed the door, Sarah asked Carl and Cherish to take a seat and returned to her seat across the table from them.

"What the hell is going on, Mother?" Cherish demanded. "Kelley was a bigamist?"

"Apparently," Sarah said. "She married Pauline the year before she and I married," Sarah explained.

"I told you from the beginning she couldn't be trusted," Cherish spat out. "She seduced you and you let her."

"Shut up, Cherish," Carl snapped. "At least give Mom a chance to tell us what happened."

"Kelley was sleeping with another woman, for God's sake!"

"I didn't know about Pauline, and she didn't know about me or the two of you until a few minutes ago. I don't know why Kelley chose to live two lives, but she did and isn't in a position to explain her actions to me at the moment. I'm not particularly happy about any of this, but I can't do anything about it. I have to accept it and you will, too."

"I didn't accept it when you met her and dragged her into our lives without even asking us how we felt, and I don't accept it now," Cherish said. "It's always been a mistake."

"You don't want to hear this, Cherish, but you're going to sit there and listen for once in your life," Sarah said with barely controlled anger. "I loved Kelley Champion with every fiber of my being. She's given me, and the two of you, everything we've ever wanted or wished for. And she put up with your snide and snotty remarks and put-downs for twenty-five fucking years, Cherish. Despite that, she paid for your ballet lessons, cheerleading camps, college, and that extravagant wedding you had to have to impress Nathan's parents. She paid every damn dime, all the while knowing you hated her. She made sure she was there for every important event in your life, including Ethan's birth. You never saw how her eyes lit up when we babysat Ethan for you. Hell, she's a better grandmother than I will ever be because she has the patience of a saint." Sarah paused to catch her breath. "Is any of this getting through to you? Every car you've driven, every expensive prom dress you couldn't live without were yours because of Kelley Champion. The fact that she didn't have a penis changed nothing. Do you know how easy it would have been for her to walk away because I had children? She stayed because she loved me!

"Today, we are dis—disconnecting Kelley from the machines that have kept her body alive until I could get here. Her brain is already dead, and now we are setting her free. Neither of you have to be there for that, but you *will* spend a moment saying your final goodbyes. On the off chance she can hear you, Cherish, please say something insulting so she knows it's you."

Sarah stood up and drank from Walter's water glass to wash the dryness from her throat. She marched around the table and across the room, slamming the door on her way out. She stopped in the hallway and leaned against the wall, gulping in deep breaths to calm down her racing mind. She wasn't ready for this. She wasn't ready for it all to end. She wasn't ready to face a future alone.

SARAH WATCHED THROUGH the wall of glass as Carl leaned down and placed a kiss on Kelley's forehead and whispered in her ear while holding her hand. Kelley's bed, along with all the hospital equipment keeping her body alive had been transferred to another room to give the family some privacy for their grief. There was still so much Kelley could have taught Carl, Sarah thought. She hoped the example Kelley set would stay with him the rest of his life.

Sarah noticed that Cherish seemed unusually quiet, not her usual snotty, spoiled self, and that scared Sarah a little. When Carl stepped back from the bed, Cherish pulled her cell phone from her pocket and punched in a number. She spoke into the phone a moment later and then brought the phone down and pressed it against Kelley's ear. Then she snapped the phone closed and whispered something to the woman she had spent a lifetime hating. When she stood up, Cherish took Carl's hand and they walked out of the room.

"Do you want me with you?" Carl asked his mother.

"No, I need this time with her," Sarah answered. She looked at Pauline who was leaning against the wall across from the room. "Are you ready?"

"No, but it is time," Pauline said.

"What was with the phone?" Sarah asked Cherish before she accompanied Pauline to say her final goodbye.

"Ethan wanted to tell his grandmother goodbye," Cherish said with a shrug.

Sarah drew Cherish into a warm embrace and whispered, "Thank you."

Sarah and Pauline followed Dr. Gilgannon and a nurse into Kelley's room. The nurse closed the Venetian blinds on the window into the hallway.

"I'll remove everything except the heart monitor," Dr. Gilgannon explained in a soft voice. "It shouldn't be more than a few minutes before her body fails. Do either of you have any questions?"

"Could you remove the breathing tube from her mouth completely, please?" Pauline asked.

"Of course."

Sarah stood on one side of Kelley's bed, Pauline on the other. They each grasped her hand in theirs and watched as the doctor removed the tube from Kelley's mouth. There was no sign of a gag reflex from having the tubing pulled from her throat. When Gilgannon completed his task, he stepped away from the bed and allowed Sarah and Pauline as much privacy as he could.

Sarah leaned over Kelley's body and kissed her on the lips for the last time. "I love you so much, sweetheart," she said. "You've been my life." She straightened up and watched as Pauline pressed her cheek to Kelley's and then kissed her lightly. "I will join you again one day, my love," Pauline whispered. Pauline looked up at Sarah and reached across the bed with her free hand. Sarah took it gratefully and closed her eyes in a silent prayer. She closed her eyes tighter when the monitor attached to Kelley emitted a solid tone to indicate her heart was no longer beating.

"No," Sarah muttered under her breath. "Not yet."

"She's gone," Gilgannon said in the quiet of the room. "Time of death five forty-seven p.m."

Sarah finally opened her eyes and reached down to run her

fingers through Kelley's short hair again. She looked up and saw the tears on Pauline's cheeks. "It's too much," she said.

Pauline wiped her tears away. "She is at peace and knew we were with her."

"You think so?"

"Yes," Pauline said. "It is that belief that will make the days to come bearable." She released Sarah's hand and together the two wives of Kelley Champion left the room.

Chapter Six

SARAH SPENT THE next two days alone as much as possible, thinking, remembering, wishing. The night she let Kelley go, she took a long walk along the city streets, watching life going on around her, wondering if the people she saw realized how lucky they were to be alive, hoping they cherished every moment. An hour later she returned to her hotel room, ordered a light meal from room service, and sat by the window in her room and allowed herself to indulge in self-pity. She needed to get the waves of grief out of her body before her life could return to a semblance of normality, if it ever did. She had barely heard Walter's voice when he read the provisions of Kelley's will. Kelley had done what she always had; the way she had always done the important things in her life. Even with her death she had provided for the people who shared her life. She could have used her money for her own pleasure and enjoyment, but chose to provide for those she left behind.

Sarah ate her dinner at a leisurely pace and leaned her head onto the back of the chair. The twinkling lights of downtown Vancouver soothed her in some way. Finally, she rose from the chair and began undressing, not planning to get up the next morning until she awoke on her own. In the two days since she'd arrived in Vancouver she had gone through a gamut of emotions, from anger to unbearable sadness, and now her body needed rest.

As she stood under the hot spray of the hotel shower, Sarah hoped the water would wash away the turmoil of the past few days. She watched as the rivulets ran down her body, between her rounded breasts, and over the rise of the middle-aged abdomen she wished she could make magically disappear. She blinked away the water which now mingled with her tears. She turned the shower massage nozzle to an intermittent pulse and let it beat down on her head and upper back. It was relaxing and felt good. Almost without realizing what she was doing she took the showerhead from its holder and swung it around over her body, feeling the soothing pulse beat against her skin as she slowly lowered it. When she felt the sensation of the pulses along the insides of her thighs, she parted her legs slightly and allowed the water to strike the most sensitive part of her body, enjoying the intensity and sexual arousal the teasing fingers of water created. She leaned her head back and could hear Kelley's voice softly in her ear. *"You're so beautiful, baby.*

I'm the luckiest woman in the world because you're mine." She gasped, startled by what she felt. She pulled the showerhead quickly away and replaced it in its holder, her hands shaking slightly. She readjusted the spray to gentle, turned the faucet off, and toweled off briskly before returning to her room and crawling into the warmth of her bed.

Sarah felt better the next morning even though she awakened only thirty minutes later than usual. With a glance at the clock on the nightstand, she rolled out of bed and stretched. She and Walter would take Carl and Cherish to the airport around noon. They both offered to remain in Vancouver with her, but she rejected their offers. She would wait with Walter and fly home on Monday.

PAULINE HAD DECIDED, after she returned from the hospital the night before, to close her store for a few days. Dressed in jeans and a lightweight sweater, she went down the stairs from her apartment. She walked into the storage room and picked up a large wreath. Her fingertips brushed over it and suddenly she hated what it represented. After the doctor told her there was no hope that Kelley would survive the stroke that had destroyed her brain, Pauline stopped at a nearby florist and ordered the mourning wreath.

Almost as soon as Kelley began living with Pauline above the little bookstore, she had begun going to the other stores close by and had become friends with most of the shop owners. Pauline was surprised when she opened the front door of her business to hang the wreath. Small tokens of remembrance from the shop owners around her had been left on the doorstep over night. Pauline knelt down and looked at each of them. Some reflected memories about Kelley's interaction with those around her. Tears came to her eyes when she picked up a small bouquet of flowers and read the attached card. Of all the people around them, Kelley had made friends with everyone except Frances Tolbert, the owner of the tobacco shop across the street from the bookstore. Now, even he acknowledged Pauline's loss. She inhaled the fresh scent of the flowers for a moment before returning the bouquet to its place among the other mementoes. She stood and hung the shrouded wreath on a hook on the door. She placed a small notice beneath it announcing the store would be closed until the following Monday. As she turned to close the door and relock it, she caught a glimpse of Frances Tolbert through the window of his tobacco shop. He raised a hand to acknowledge her and turned quickly away.

TWO DAYS LATER Pauline stepped from the back seat of a taxi, holding a medium-sized package in her hands. She leaned down and handed the fare to the driver before turning to face the front entrance of the hotel. The doorman opened the glass door for her and she approached the front desk, waiting for the clerk to contact Sarah. If Sarah refused to see her, Pauline would be forced to leave the package with the clerk. After a brief telephone conversation the clerk told Pauline the room number and that Mrs. Champion was expecting her. Pauline nodded her gratitude and clutched the package closer to her body as she walked toward the elevator.

She looked out over the city as the glass-enclosed elevator rose smoothly up the outside of the hotel. She hoped she had made a wise decision. She knew it was the right thing to do. She was still stunned from learning Kelley had been married to another woman and stroked the top of the box with her thumbs. The elevator doors slid open, and she stepped into the carpeted hallway, looking at the plaques posted on the wall before turning toward the room she was looking for. The room was at the end of a long hallway and had double doors. Pauline saw a doorbell on the right-hand side. She pressed the bell and stepped back a little to wait.

The sound of the door being unlocked drew Pauline's attention back to the reason she had come to the fashionable hotel. A tentative smile she didn't really feel appeared automatically on her face as the door cracked open. The woman standing before her now looked tired and haggard. Dark circles were beginning to form beneath Sarah's eyes and the semi-cheerful look faded quickly from Pauline's face.

"I'm sorry," she said. "I hope I haven't interrupted anything."

"No, no," Sarah said. "I was just indulging in a little self-pity. I wasn't expecting anyone. What can I do for you?"

Pauline felt awkward and wondered once again if she'd made the right decision. "I— um—I brought you this," she said as she thrust the package toward Sarah.

"What is this?" Sarah frowned.

Pauline shifted nervously from one foot to the other, searching for the best way to tell Sarah what was in the package. Finally she took a deep breath and decided to simply spit it out. There was no way to make what she had to say any easier. "After Kelley was cremated I asked the mortuary to divide her ashes into two containers. This one is yours to do with as you see fit. I shall take my half and spread them overlooking the ocean. Kelley loved it there."

As quickly as she had said what she needed to say, Pauline shut up. Sarah stared at the package in her hands, but said nothing.

"Well, that's all I have to say," Pauline said and turned to leave.

"Wait!" Sarah called out. "I apologize. This is something I never expected. I had already said my goodbyes. This is...this is very generous of you."

"There's no generosity involved. It is simply the right thing to do, and Kelley would have expected nothing less from me."

"Would you care to come in?" Sarah asked as she visibly relaxed. "I'll order some coffee from room service."

Pauline expelled a breath and allowed the tightness in her face to relax. "I would *love* a cup of coffee," she said.

Pauline followed Sarah into the room and looked around. "This is very nice," she commented.

Sarah carried the box to the table next to the window and opened it to reveal a small ceramic container, letting her finger linger on it for a moment. "Let me order our coffee," she said.

As she waited for Sarah to place her order with room service, Pauline's eyes tracked around the front room of the hotel suite. Her eyes were drawn to a framed photograph on the mantle over the faux fireplace. She moved to the mantle and picked up the picture. Tears welled up in her eyes as she gazed down at the smiling face of Kelley Champion. She was wearing a sweater and jeans over her familiar hiking boots. Happiness exuded from the picture of Kelley looking into Sarah's eyes. They were the picture of contentment and lasting love.

"A friend took that picture a couple of years ago," Sarah's voice said from behind Pauline. "It's my favorite picture of Kelley."

"She...you both look very happy," Pauline managed as she set the picture back on the mantle. She turned to face Sarah. "This is incredibly awkward for me," she said. "My mind says I should be furious, but my heart won't allow it." Before Sarah could say anything the bell to the suite rang announcing the arrival of their coffee. The waiter rolled a small cart into the room and poured two cups. Sarah handed one to Pauline as the waiter left the room.

Pauline sat in a wingback chair on one side of the fireplace while Sarah curled her feet beneath her on the loveseat. They both sipped their coffee quietly for a few minutes.

"I wouldn't blame you if you were angry," Sarah said. "I can understand that. One day I am a happily married woman and the next, I am 'the other woman.' I don't know how I'm supposed to feel about any of this. I think, in some way, I am angry with Kelley. At this terrible situation she has left us in." She took a sip of her coffee and closed her eyes to savor its taste. "I can't believe I never saw a hint that she led two separate lives," she said. Then she became pensive. "Maybe I did and ignored it because I didn't want to deal with it."

"When will you return home?" Pauline asked.

"Walter has some business here, but we plan to fly back to Boston early Monday."

Pauline looked at Sarah and knew why Kelley had loved her. Dressed in jeans and a long-sleeved t-shirt, Sarah was the picture of casual wholesomeness. Suddenly she felt uncomfortable being alone in the hotel suite with Sarah and stood up. "I don't want to take up any more of your time," she said.

Pauline crossed the room to pick up her shoulder bag and caught a glimpse of the bedroom. Sudden anger and jealousy flared in her mind as she pictured Kelley in the room making love to Sarah. She slammed her eyes shut to block the image from her mind. She turned toward the door of the suite and struggled not to show what she was feeling. She should hate the woman facing her, but she didn't. Sarah had been as blissfully ignorant as she had been. Pauline held out her hand and said, "I wish you well in the future, Sarah."

"I wish the same for you," Sarah replied as she followed Pauline to the door and opened it.

"I was wondering," Pauline stopped and said. "There is a place Kelley loved on Vancouver Island. She could sit for hours and watch the waves break against the cliffs. I was thinking perhaps I would spread her ashes there."

"I'm sure she would like that," Sarah said.

"Would you like to accompany me?" Pauline asked. "I have closed my store until next week and could go this weekend. It wouldn't delay your trip home."

"I don't know," Sarah hesitated.

"You have your children who will accompany you. I do not. I would appreciate the company. That is, if you're willing. I understand if it would make you too uncomfortable. It was just a thought." Pauline's voice began to fade away the more she spoke.

"When would you go?" Sarah asked.

"The sun setting into the ocean is magnificent. After lunch tomorrow, perhaps. It is quite a long trip, about three hours one way. We should be back in the city before midnight."

"Midnight!"

"The last ferry departs for the mainland at nine. There is no other way to get there. If we missed the ferry we would be forced to spend the night on the island."

"That's fine," Sarah finally capitulated.

"I will meet you in front of your hotel around four then," Pauline said.

SARAH SLIPPED HER sunglasses on and leaned her head back on the passenger seat of Pauline's Hyundai Santa Fe. She relaxed as Pauline drove to the ferry terminal just north of the city. They waited in line to load the car onto the ferry that would take them across the Straits of Georgia to Vancouver Island. The ceramic container holding half of Kelley's ashes sat mutely between them.

"It's beautiful here," Sarah said once they were out of the vehicle and enjoying the breeze coming off the water during the thirty mile journey across the strait.

"Kelley loved it," Pauline commented almost to herself. "In the winter, we would sometimes spend a weekend in the mountains skiing or just relaxing away from work." Pauline said. "She could find something good no matter how badly a trip turned out. I've never met anyone so perpetually, or annoyingly, happy."

"She enjoyed life," Sarah said.

"It seems unfair that someone who enjoyed life as much as she did should lose it so early."

Sarah thought for a minute. "Perhaps that's why she enjoyed it so much. She knew it could end without warning."

"Do you enjoy life, Sarah?" Pauline asked. Her eyes quickly glanced at Sarah before returning to scan the water. She noticed that Sarah seemed a little more relaxed than she had the day before. Her blonde hair and her features seemed to glow from the reflection of the sun upon the water.

"I did after I met Kelley. Not so much before that. I don't know what I'll do now without her with me."

"Do you work?"

"Kelley hired me twenty-six years ago for a position at Bilt-Rite. After we began making a life together, she insisted I stop working and take care of our home and the children."

"What did you do when she was traveling?"

"When Carl and Cherish were younger their schedules kept me busy. I did some volunteer work for our favorite charities. What did you do?"

"I have the bookstore and spent some time going to dinner with friends when she was away. There were many times I wished Kelley was there when I had a problem, but she was proud of the way I worked through them myself. She wanted me to be independent."

Silence fell over both women as they became immersed in their own thoughts. Almost an hour and a half later, Pauline drove off the ferry and turned toward the town of Nanaimo where they would pick up the highway leading to the west coast of the island. The sun was low in the western sky when Pauline swung the SUV into a parking space next to a small stone building and turned the ignition off.

"What is this building?" Sarah asked.

"It once was a church, but they stopped having services here two or three years ago. Kelly and I were married here," Pauline answered softly. She reached into the vehicle and picked up the ceramic container. She pushed the door closed, pointed to a path leading into a thick stand of trees and said, "We're going up there. We will have to walk a little bit, but it's not difficult terrain."

Sarah shielded her eyes from the sun and began following Pauline up a path that had been carved through the trees. Pauline stopped after several hundred yards and left the path, Sarah close behind. Sarah followed her across a long suspension walkway over a deep ravine. Lush, green foliage covered the ground as far as Sarah could see. The canopy of old growth trees overhead cast deep shadows over everything. Just as Sarah was wondering how much farther Pauline would lead her, they stepped out of the trees and into a small meadow that led to a rocky outcropping and onto a white, sandy beach.

The setting sun hovered near the top of the blue ocean that extended away from the land as far as Sarah could see. Rays of sunlight shimmered across the top of the waves rushing toward the shore below them. Birds flew overhead calling out their farewell to another day.

"Look!" Sarah exclaimed as she pointed toward the ocean. The distinctive black and white markings of two killer whales broke the water's surface playfully. "Oh, my God, what a breathtaking sight," Sarah breathed.

"It is a perfect day," Pauline said. She climbed to the top of the tallest boulder and stood quietly as a light ocean spray flew around her. She lifted the lid from the container in her hands and waited only a moment. As the whales broke the water once again, a light breeze moved up the sides of the rocky outcropping and ruffled her hair. Pauline tilted the container slightly and let the wind catch the ashes inside as they fell. Both women watched them as they swirled and were carried away. Sarah saw tears running down Pauline's cheeks, but there was no sadness on her face. When the container was empty, they sat on the beach and watched the sun slip farther into the water.

"She was happy here, and now she is a part of it," Pauline said softly. She turned her head toward Sarah. "Thank you for sharing this with me."

Sarah reached out and squeezed Pauline's arm lightly. "I was honored. Perhaps I'll come back here one day to remember her."

"She would like that," Pauline said.

EARLY MONDAY MORNING Sarah walked next to Walter down the concourse toward their gate. It would feel good to return to her home and more familiar surroundings. Although she didn't know what she would do with herself alone in the large three-story brownstone, she would have to think of something. She was only fifty-three years old and reasonably assumed she still had several good years ahead of her. Perhaps she would get a dog to keep her company and turn into one of those little old blue-haired ladies who tried to sneak their small pets into grocery stores and restaurants. She knew she wasn't dead yet and was equally certain she would never know the passion she had experienced with Kelley with anyone again, but there was more to life than physical intimacy. Wasn't there?

Not trusting the airline baggage handlers, Sarah had packed her ceramic container into her carry-on bag. Even if she lost everything else she owned, she wouldn't lose that. Winter weather would begin sweeping across the northern United States in a few weeks. Before it became impossible to reach their cabin in Vermont, she would drive north and repeat the process she had shared with Pauline outside of Vancouver. The more she thought about it, the more she thought it was a moment she should share with Pauline. Carl and Cherish only knew the public woman Kelley had been. Only she and Pauline knew the private, intimate woman.

"May I borrow your cell phone, Walter?" she asked as they took seats in the gate waiting area.

"Of course, my dear. Are you all right?"

"Yes, I'm fine," she said as she took the phone and stood. "I'll be right back."

"Don't wander too far away. They'll be calling our flight in a few minutes," Walter warned.

"I'm not a child, Walter," Sarah said. A hint of the irritation she still harbored toward him was evident in her voice.

Walter pulled out the newspaper he had taken from the hotel and laughed to himself as she walked across the concourse to place her call. She flipped the phone open and punched an icon to display Walter's contact list. She scrolled down until she found Pauline Champion's phone number and connected to it. When a voice said, *"Bon jour,"* Sarah almost disconnected. Just suck it up, she thought. It's for Kelley, she told herself.

"Hello, Pauline?" Sarah said into the small device pressed against her ear.

"Yes, this is Pauline Champion. May I assist you?"

"Pauline, this is Sarah."

"You are home already?"

"No, I'm at the Vancouver airport. Our flight is leaving soon.

Pauline, would you consider flying to Massachusetts and going with me to spread Kelley's ashes?"

Silence from the other end of the phone made Sarah wonder if the call had been dropped. "Pauline?" she asked.

"I am sorry, Sarah. I had to open the front door for my clerk. When would you go?"

"I need a little time. Could you come in two weeks?"

Sarah heard the airport intercom announce that her flight was beginning the boarding process. "Look, they've called my flight and I have to go before Walter has a stro...," she started to say. "I'm sorry. That was a thoughtless thing to say. Just think about it, and I'll call you back when I get home. I'll send you a ticket if..."

"No. I can afford my own ticket. I can fly in Friday afternoon and arrange a flight back to Vancouver for Sunday. Is that acceptable?"

"Thank you, Pauline. I appreciate it very much."

"It is the least I can do for Kelley. I'll let you know what time my flight arrives."

A glance up revealed a frantically waving Walter who was allowing other passengers to board ahead of him. "Do you have a pen and paper? My number is 617-555-4440. I have to go now."

"Have a safe flight," Pauline said, her soft voice flowing smoothly over Sarah's ear.

Sarah flipped the phone shut and trotted across the concourse to join Walter.

Chapter Seven

SARAH PARKED HER copper-colored Nissan Murano in the closest spot she could find to the Air Canada terminal at Logan International Airport two weeks later. She walked quickly toward the terminal, checking her wristwatch nervously. She didn't want to be late, but an accident on the freeway had stalled traffic for more than half an hour. She glanced around inside and located the sign that directed her to baggage claims. She stepped onto the escalator and rode it to the ground level, stopping only to check the arrival and departure boards overhead. Flight 2254 was listed as on time and scheduled to arrive in less than ten minutes. In airport jargon that probably meant the flight was already on the ground and taxiing toward its gate, Sarah thought. She'd made it with very little time to spare. Pauline would have to stop at customs to present her passport, but visitors from Canada rarely had difficulty getting through the checkpoint.

Despite her best efforts to calm down, Sarah danced around from foot to foot and watched passengers moving down the escalators toward baggage claims. It had been a difficult two weeks emotionally. A ringing bell announcing the arrival of luggage from a flight startled Sarah and she looked over her shoulder to see AC2254 light up above carousel number two. She returned her attention to the escalators and spotted Pauline's auburn hair. Sarah waved until she caught Pauline's attention and met her next to the support pillar near the escalator.

It had only been two weeks since Sarah had seen Pauline, but she couldn't seem to escape the feeling of happiness seeing her again brought. Despite the awkward situation they were in, Sarah was forced to acknowledge that she liked Pauline, probably more than she should.

"Was your flight okay?" Sarah asked when Pauline stopped in front of her.

"Not bad, except for the horrible movie they showed," Pauline answered. She held up her hand. "Good thing I brought a good book," she laughed lightly.

The sound of Pauline's laughter made Sarah swallow hard before she could speak again. Why the hell am I thinking about that? Sarah asked herself. I just lost the woman who meant more to me than anything in the world, and now I can't stop ogling her other 'wife.' Ridiculous!

"I thought we might stop for lunch, unless airplane food has improved in the last two weeks, and then drive straight to the cabin. It's about a three-hour drive if the traffic's good."

"Since I know nothing about the area, I'm placing myself completely in your hands," Pauline said.

Oh, God, Sarah groaned to herself as Pauline leaned over the carousel to pick up her small suitcase. She forced herself to avert her eyes to keep from staring at Pauline's ass, which filled out her jeans perfectly.

"DO YOU LIKE this car?" Pauline asked as she fastened her seatbelt in the Murano.

"I thought it was too expensive when Kelley bought it last year, but now I've been spoiled by how well it handles on the road. Overall, I think it's as comfortable as your Santa Fe."

Pauline laughed. "It seems we can't talk about anything that Kelley isn't a part of. She bought our car because she thought we needed more room for camping equipment."

"She was a major part of both our lives, and I'm afraid she can't be avoided," Sarah said.

"Rather like the very large elephant in the room that everyone tries not to be the first to mention."

"I'm sure she'd love being compared to a large elephant," Sarah laughed out loud.

Sarah guided her car north toward the Massachusetts state line and set the cruise control before settling down in the driver's seat. "We'll have to stop in Montpelier to pick up a few groceries. Everything in the cabin is working, but the refrigerator is completely empty. What kind of food do you like?"

"I'm not a picky eater. Whatever you like is fine." Pauline gazed out the passenger window and watched the countryside change from city, to suburbs, and finally to trees as far as the eyes could see when they crossed into Vermont. The trees had changed into their fall colors and she was surrounded by a canopy of reds, oranges, and yellows, as well as half a dozen shades in between.

"This is the best time of year in the northeast. I wish the fall colors lasted longer, but we could be buried in snow in a few weeks," Sarah said. "Then this area will be overrun with tourists and locals trying to get to the ski resorts. We stopped going to the cabin in the winter after the kids got over their ski mania. They come up occasionally, but life is too busy for them to make the trip very often."

"It's beautiful," Pauline said.

"The cabin has a wrap-around deck. You can walk completely

around the outside and see nothing but trees. I know the perfect spot to spread my half of the ashes, but we'll have to get up before daylight to get there at the right time."

"Then we'll have to go to bed early tonight."

Please don't say something like that, Sarah thought. *Maybe I should have come here alone.* Suddenly, Sarah needed some cool fresh air and stopped at a grocery chain in Montpelier. They only needed enough food to get through Sunday morning when they would drive back to Boston. Pauline had booked a flight for seven Sunday evening. Considering the time difference between Boston and Vancouver, she would arrive home not much later than the time she left.

Before pushing her cart to the check-out line, Sarah picked up a couple of bottles of wine and added them to her groceries. She had no doubt she would need something to help her relax over the next couple of days.

The sun had dropped to the top of the tree line along the Green Mountains when Sarah turned the Murano onto a single-lane, blacktopped drive into the mountains overlooking Stowe, Vermont. She pulled the car under a wooden canopy that made up the main deck that ran around the cabin.

Pauline stepped out of the vehicle and looked around at the gardens still blooming at the edge of a grassy lawn that ended at the tree line. "When you said cabin, I was thinking something a little smaller and more rustic," she said over the top of the car. "This is almost a mansion."

Sarah laughed and opened the rear door to pull out their groceries while Pauline opened the back hatch and took out their luggage. "Kelley called it the cabin. Now that she's gone, I won't be making many trips here anymore. I'm thinking about selling it next year."

"Why?"

"Too many memories to be alone with here. I wouldn't be able to enjoy it if I was crying all the damn time," Sarah answered with a shrug.

Sarah set the groceries on the kitchen counter and showed Pauline to a guest bedroom that overlooked the valley below. A sliding glass door opened onto the deck and the room had a separate bathroom. "I think you should be comfortable in here. Our room is at the opposite end of the house so we won't have to worry about disturbing one another."

Sarah took food from the grocery bags and began placing them in the cabinets and refrigerator. She started a pot of coffee before rolling her small suitcase into the master bedroom and hoisting it onto the bed. She wouldn't need many clothes for the two days they would be at the cabin, and it only took her a few minutes to put everything away. She closed her suitcase and rolled it into the closet out of the way.

She took a moment to sit on Kelley's side of the bed and run her fingers over it. She pulled the bedspread down far enough to grab the pillow and hold it against her. The scent of Kelley filled her lungs. It would always be there, no matter how many times she changed the sheets. Kelley was everywhere around her, and Sarah missed her more than she could believe. She shook her head and replaced the pillow carefully before returning to the kitchen.

The coffeemaker burbled and spit out the last of the coffee into the carafe. She poured two cups and sipped the hot liquid. It would be dark soon and everything around the cabin would fall silent until the sun rose again. She looked out the kitchen window and saw Pauline leaning back in a deck chair with one foot propped against the deck railing. She picked up both cups of coffee and carried them through the breakfast area sliding door.

"It will start to get quite cool out here once the sun falls behind the mountains," she said as she set a cup next to Pauline.

"Thank you," Pauline said, picking up the cup and holding it in both hands to absorb the warmth of the coffee.

"Is everything all right in your room?"

"Yes. Very nice and this is so peaceful."

"Kelley's father was in the lumber business. He bought this section of land and wouldn't let anyone build nearby. Kelley was offered quite a bit of money for a parcel of land farther down, but refused to sell it. She liked the solitude." A grin cut across Sarah's face. "And she liked being able to run around in just her scivvies or less."

"Scivvies?"

"Her underwear."

Pauline laughed as she brought her cup to her mouth. "I can picture that very easily."

Sarah looked out at the darkness settling over the trees and stood up. "I'll get dinner in the oven. I assume you know how to start a fire."

"Yes. Kel-," Pauline started.

"She taught me how to start a fire, too," Sarah interrupted.

As Sarah prepared a simple chicken and rice casserole, she glanced up from time to time to watch Pauline squatting in front of the fireplace. Everything seemed so normal. It was as if Kelley was there again, starting a fire while she prepared dinner. But Pauline wasn't Kelley. In fact, she was nothing like Kelley, except that she was a nice, friendly woman who was easy to be around.

SARAH WOKE UP the next morning before the alarm clock next to her buzzed. She drew the belt of her robe around her waist and made her way into the kitchen. She turned on the coffeemaker to let coffee brew while she took a quick shower and got dressed. By the time she finished drying her hair and walked out of her bedroom, she smelled the freshly brewed coffee. Apparently so had Pauline, who was in the process of filling two mugs.

"Good morning," Sarah said. "Did I wake you?"

"No, I'm a light sleeper and the delicious smell of this coffee attacked my nose," Pauline said with a smile.

"I can scramble some eggs if you want to eat before we leave," Sarah offered.

"I can wait until we return. Then I can eat at a more leisurely pace."

Sarah took two travel mugs from the cabinet and handed one to Pauline. "It might still be pretty chilly outside and we'll need this," she said as she poured her coffee into the insulated cup and topped it off.

Hot coffee in hand, Pauline and Sarah went down the stairs and got into Sarah's car. Once again, Kelley's ashes sat between them in a ceramic container. Sarah backed the Murano up and drove down the blacktop to the highway. A few miles down the road she signaled to turn onto a narrow two-lane road that led into the mountains.

"Mt. Mansfield is the highest peak in Vermont," she said. "It's not exactly the Rocky Mountains, but it's the best we have around here. This road doesn't take us to the top, but there's a hiking trail that goes the rest of the way. This particular trail isn't too demanding. Kelley and I have hiked them all, mostly when we were much younger," she said as she negotiated the first of several hairpin turns along the road.

A paved parking area signaled the end of the road. Sarah got out of the car, taking the ceramic container with her. She opened the back hatch and took out two flashlights that cast a powerful beam along the trail in front of them. They climbed at a steady pace, stopping periodically to catch their breath and drink a little coffee to warm up. Finally, Sarah looked up and could see the silhouette of the top of the mountain against the sky that was beginning to lighten.

"We're almost there," she told Pauline over her shoulder.

"Is this a payback for making you walk up to the cliffs in Vancouver?" Pauline asked.

"No. That wasn't as steep or as far as this."

Sarah shined her flashlight around and located a large flat boulder. She sat down gratefully and pulled her legs up to sit cross-legged. Pauline sat down next to her and let her legs dangle over the side of the boulder. The quiet wrapped them in a cocoon of darkness as they waited.

Sarah felt around and found small rocks near where she was seated. She picked them up and played with them. "Originally, I was going to spread the ashes at the cabin. You know, no big deal," she said. "But after Vancouver I decided to bring Kelley here. You spread her ashes over the cliffs and the ocean to mix with the setting sun. If I spread her ashes here over the mountain to greet the rising sun, it will be kind of like completing a circle. Every time the sun rises, I will think about her and know she's a part of it," Sarah said.

"And I will think of her with every sunset," Pauline said softly. "It is perfect, Sarah."

"Look," Sarah said pointing toward the east. "It's not as good as the whales, but it's a sign that a new day is beginning." She stood and took a deep breath as she watched a line of light move slowly across the valley below, driving the shadow of night before it. They watched the daylight move steadily toward them. Slowly it crept up the side of the mountain until it was just below their feet. Sarah removed the top of the container and held it in front of her. She looked down and saw the edge of light hit her feet and begin to climb up her shins, then her thighs. Warmth from the light felt soothing against her legs. As soon as the light reached her abdomen she tilted the container and watched the ashes scatter down and across the side of the mountain. "Fly free, my darling," she murmured. "Come back to me each morning." When the container was empty, Sarah dropped it from her hands and covered her eyes, releasing every pent-up emotion inside. She fell to her knees and bent at the waist as sobs overcame her. Pauline knelt beside her and wrapped an arm around her shoulders, allowing Sarah to rid herself of the grief that only Pauline could understand.

AFTER A QUIET drive back to the cabin, Sarah excused herself and went into her bedroom. The finality of her loss had stricken her on Mt. Mansfield that morning and left her completely and utterly drained emotionally. She thought she could handle the final farewell and had been wrong. She was embarrassed she had broken down in front of Pauline. She lay back on the bed, too exhausted to do anything other than fall asleep.

The next time Sarah opened her eyes she felt better, but was still groggy when she sat up and swung her feet off the bed. She rubbed her eyes when she saw the time on her bedside clock. She walked quickly to the closest window and threw back the drapes.

The sun was obviously setting. She had slept the whole day. Sarah hurriedly put on her tennis shoes and tied the laces. As she rushed into the kitchen, there were no other lights on inside the cabin. She looked out the kitchen window, but didn't see Pauline anywhere. She made her way down the hallway to the other end of the cabin and breathed a sigh of relief when she saw the dim slit of light from under the guest room door. She cracked the door open and saw Pauline sprawled on her bed, glasses halfway down her nose, and an open book lying across her abdomen.

Satisfied she wasn't alone Sarah closed the door quietly and returned to the kitchen. She chopped ingredients for a salad and wrapped two medium potatoes in aluminum foil. She took two six-ounce steaks from the refrigerator and prepared them for the grill. When the pre-heat timer on the oven dinged, she popped the potatoes inside.

She started a fire in the grill on the deck and another small cozy fire in the fireplace in the cabin's main room. She could feel the chill in the air while she was getting the grill ready and knew the fire inside would feel good later that evening. She cut up apples, bananas, pineapple, and fresh blueberries for dessert and poured a sauce made of powdered sugar and cream over them. She pulled down two plates and carried them, along with silverware and napkins, to a table near the fireplace. The fire was small enough to make the room comfortable. She took a candleholder from the mantle and set it between the two plates. She would cook the steaks slowly over a medium heat to keep their juices inside. If she timed it right, the potatoes would be ready when she brought the steaks in.

PAULINE HEARD SARAH approaching the guest room and closed her eyes, pretending to be sound asleep when Sarah peeked into the room. Pauline had stopped reading nearly an hour earlier and rested the book on her stomach. Her mind was too pre-occupied to pay much attention to what she was reading. She had been surprised by Sarah's emotional disintegration that morning on the mountain. Sarah had lived with Kelley ten years longer than she had and undoubtedly knew her much better. Pauline had never questioned where Kelley went or what she did between her stays in Vancouver. Why would she? She trusted Kelley implicitly, just as Sarah had.

Sarah was a wonderful woman and apparently lived to make Kelley's every wish come true. Despite herself and her love for Kelley, Pauline hadn't been able to stop small flirtations with Sarah. She never seemed offended by Pauline's remarks, but perhaps that was simply her way of taking everything in stride. But Sarah hadn't been able to take her final moments with all that remained of Kelley in stride as she saw the last tangible pieces of her float away. It was obvious to Pauline that Sarah was heartbroken, devastated, when forced to finally say goodbye.

Clearly, Kelley had chosen well when she found Sarah twenty-five years earlier. She was a gentle soul as well as an attractive and desirable woman. Tomorrow, Pauline thought, I will board a plane to Vancouver, and Sarah will be out of my life. We were thrown together by a heartbreaking tragedy and have only shared a few days together. Tomorrow would be the first day of the rest of their lives, and they owed it to Kelley to continue to lead happy lives. Was she wrong to find another woman desirable so soon after her loss? She had never been unfaithful to Kelley. Was her attraction to Sarah now being unfaithful to her memory or a way of being close to her again?

Pauline sat up and went into the bathroom. She washed her face, brushed her teeth, and ran a comb through her hair. When she entered the kitchen she saw a bottle of wine on the counter, opened to allow it to breathe. She found two wine glasses in a cabinet over the sink. She looked at the wine label and recognized it as one Kelley had favored. She paused before filling each glass halfway. When she opened the door onto the deck, Sarah flipped the steaks over and closed the top on the grill to keep the heat inside.

"These should be ready in a few minutes," she said.

Pauline extended a glass to Sarah and took a sip of her own wine. Sarah took the glass gratefully and let out a hum of satisfaction as she took a drink. "Did you have a good nap?" Sarah asked. "I think we both needed one. I didn't mean to sleep the day away."

"How do you feel?" Pauline asked.

Sarah thought for a moment. "Much better, actually. This morning was more stressful than I thought it would be, but I don't know why."

Ten minutes later Pauline slid the glass door open and Sarah carried a platter inside. "I hope your steak is the way you like it. I didn't want to wake you up to ask," Sarah said as she carried the platter to the table. "Will you get the salad from the refrigerator while I check the potatoes? Take whatever dressing you prefer and grab the Italian for me, please."

Satisfied they had everything they needed both women pulled their chairs closer to the table. Pauline opened the two bottles of dressing while Sarah placed a steak on each plate. Pauline got up and retrieved the wine from the kitchen counter. When she sat back down she said, "Now this is a complete meal." She refilled Sarah's glass and her own before holding her glass up for a toast. "To Kelley," she said. Sarah's glass touched hers and they both drank a healthy swallow.

"I'm starving," Sarah said. "We managed to miss breakfast and lunch today."

"Sometimes rest is more important than food," Pauline said. She cut into her steak and brought her fork to her mouth. "This is perfect, Sarah. Everything is perfect. Thank you."

They ate hungrily without much conversation for several minutes until Pauline said, "You are a wonderful cook. It must be because you had children and a wife to cook for. I'm afraid my own cooking expertise is limited to much simpler food." She laughed and shook her head in amusement. "Actually, I'm a terrible cook," she said, leaning partially across the table as if divulging a secret. "Kelley did almost all the cooking when she was home. Did that make me a horrible wife?"

Sarah washed down her last bite with her wine before she replied. "Of course not. Kelley enjoyed cooking and experimenting in the kitchen. It was something we could do together while we talked over the events of our day."

"I've eaten more than one of Kelley's experiments," Pauline said. "Some were more successful than others."

"That's why I always had a back-up meal for the kids," Sarah said with a grin.

"There is a delightful take-out place not far from our apartment," Pauline giggled. "I had their number on speed dial, just in case."

Pauline took another swallow of her wine and refilled her glass. "Are you uncomfortable talking about Kelley?" she asked as she offered more to wine to Sarah.

Sarah held her glass out and shook her head. "I thought I would be, but I'm not. Talking about her brings back so many memories, both good and bad. I think it's a healthy process to deal with how I feel. I threw together a fruit salad for dessert."

"No, no. I am quite full now. Perhaps later. Since you did all the cooking, let me clean up so we can relax."

"I won't argue with that," Sarah said as she started to get up.

"You rest and leave this part to me," Pauline said as she stood next to Sarah and placed a hand on her shoulder.

Sarah nodded and leaned back in her chair, watching as Pauline made several trips back and forth between the table and the kitchen. It seemed as if no time at all had passed before Pauline announced everything was taken care of. She returned to the table carrying the second bottle of wine. "This fire is very inviting," she said. She pulled two large floor pillows closer to the fireplace and settled on one, motioning for Sarah to join her. When Sarah was comfortably ensconced on the second pillow, Pauline asked, "What is you favorite memory of Kelley?"

"That's easy," Sarah said, "but I'm not sure I can talk about it."

"Ah, an intimate moment," Pauline said softly.

Sarah nodded and Pauline saw the color in her face become darker as it reddened slightly in the flickering firelight.

Pauline cleared her throat. "I am sure we both have such memories," she said as she looked into the fire and watched small flames jump and lick at the burning wood.

"Did she call you every day?" Sarah asked.

"Every day at lunchtime," Pauline said. "When she was in Boston, her lunchtime was early in the morning, Vancouver time."

"She called from her office?"

"Yes."

"What if you needed her...for an emergency?"

"I paged her at first. We used a code so she would know it was important that we speak. We devised a numeric page just to say I love you during the day."

Sarah frowned and stared into her glass of wine. "We did the same things. Even if she received a page while we were together, even on vacation with the children, I wouldn't have suspected a thing. The stores paged her all the time."

"I remember," Pauline said as she sipped her wine. "Where did you go on your vacations?"

"Never to the west coast, except on our honeymoon. She said she already spent so much time there, she didn't want to return for a vacation. Now I know why," Sarah said bitterly. She noticed Pauline was beginning to look a little uncomfortable. "I'm sorry. It wasn't your fault." She took a deep breath. "Kelley took us on cruises, mostly to the various islands in the Caribbean. One summer we flew to New Zealand to ski. The kids were amazed because the seasons were reversed," Sarah said. "What about you?"

"I'm afraid I'm not much of a world traveler. We camped when the weather was warm and skied in the winter. She bought tickets for the Olympics one winter. That was a wonderful trip."

"Why did she do it? Why wasn't I enough for her? Why did she have to turn to another woman for satisfaction?" Sarah asked, her voice becoming harder with each question. Pauline leaned against the couch and let Sarah speak. Sarah gulped down the wine remaining in her glass. "I gave her everything. My love, my devotion, my body. And yet it wasn't enough after a while. You're a beautiful woman, Pauline, and I can't fault you for falling in love with Kelley. It was her. She was very easy to love. But, she betrayed me. She betrayed both of us." Tears began to fill Sarah's eyes. They hovered along her lower eyelids before a blink forced them out. She brushed them away angrily and took a deep breath to regain control of her emotions. "I'm sorry," she muttered. "I promised myself I wouldn't do this."

"We need to," Pauline replied. "I can't let my doubts and hurt feelings fill me and fester. I wouldn't expect you to either."

"Why didn't I know about you?" Sarah asked. "Other women say a wife can always tell when their spouse strays into the arms of another woman. The passion in their lovemaking changes subtly. Was I just so glad to have her with me when she came home that I didn't notice? Was I only thinking about my own needs?"

"I never suspected you existed either. I had been with other women before Kelley, and I always knew if they were cheating," Pauline said. "With Kelley, it never entered my mind."

Sarah sighed. "I don't think Kelley thought of it as cheating. In her mind you weren't 'the other woman.' You were her wife, just as I was." Sarah ran her hand over her face. "That sounds stupid even to me."

Pauline took a drink and looked at Sarah. "Do you hate me, Sarah? Because I shared a life and my bed with Kelley?"

"I did when I first saw you at the hospital. I wanted to claw your eyes out. You stole my wife from me. You seduced her and took the most precious thing in my world away. But, then I looked at you and I knew it was my fault that it happened. You're a slender, beautiful woman, and I am certainly not as slender or desirable looking. I've, um, settled over the years and assumed I didn't have to work as hard to keep Kelley's affections."

"Oh, stop it, Sarah," Pauline said harshly. "Did Kelley ever say such a thing to you or make you feel less than you are? I can see by looking around me how much she loved you."

"And yet she turned to you," Sarah snapped.

"But not at your expense. She denied you nothing and when she left my bed she returned willingly to yours. Not even your children could drive her away from your side."

"What are you talking about?" Sarah demanded at the mention of her children.

"I heard what you said to your daughter in the hospital conference room. Your voice was loud enough for me to know your daughter did everything possible to make Kelley's life with you miserable over the years. And yet, she stayed. For you. Only love can make that happen."

"When I first found out who you were from Walter, I thought you were some kind of gold digger who seduced Kelley because of her money," Sarah admitted. "In my mind I tried to make you into an evil temptress. But I knew that wasn't true the first time I heard you speak. The way you acted toward her while she was lying in the ICU wasn't the behavior of a woman who didn't care."

"Walter was the only one, other than Kelley, who knew about us both. I looked at you in the conference room and thought if what he was telling me was true, then you must have been a cold, unfeeling woman to have driven Kelley away," Pauline said as she watched the flames of the fire. "Obviously, I was wrong because I saw the hurt in your eyes. You're a beautiful woman with a gentle soul. I actually found myself feeling guilty, mostly because Kelley had betrayed you. But she betrayed me as well. I really didn't know what to think after that. I think I was jealous once I knew of the times she spent with you. I let my emotions overcome my reason. I didn't want to picture Kelley holding you in her arms or lying next to you in bed," Pauline admitted as her voice began to crack. She closed her eyes and took a deep breath. "I wondered, for a while, if what she felt when she was with you was more than she felt with me. Those thoughts drove me down into a very dark place, and I was glad she was dead."

"I thought I sensed someone in the darkness with me," Sarah said. "But now I can see the light at the top of that pit. I never want to lose my memories of Kelley, but it will take me a while to forgive her, I think."

"And what about your children now? How are they adjusting now that they know?"

Sarah leaned forward slightly and held her glass out. Pauline filled it and added more to her own.

"Carl will miss Kelley the most. They have always been close," Sarah said. "She was so proud of him when he came home with a busted lip after a fight during a junior hockey game. I didn't find out until much later that she had been teaching him how to fight," Sarah laughed. "I was furious at her, but he was such a scrawny kid and smaller than the other boys. Kelley hated seeing him being picked on and shoved around. Most of that stopped after that first fight."

"And your daughter?"

"She will feel relieved that Kelley's gone. I can't remember a day that Cherish didn't hate Kelley. It disgusted her if she saw us kiss one another." Sarah covered her eyes with her hand. "God, the poor girl would have died if she'd known what we did when we were alone." Sarah bent forward and laughter bubbled up. "I hope her sex life is half as good as ours was. Otherwise she'd be terribly jealous."

Pauline laughed as well and sipped her wine. "Children must make life interesting."

"Oh, my God!" Sarah exclaimed. "When Kelley and I first

began living together, every time we thought we had a private moment, a child interrupted us." The skin next to Sarah's eyes crinkled as she chuckled again. "Once when Carl was about fifteen or sixteen, he began to demand more of Kelley's time when she was home. Of course, she always spent a lot of time with him, but around then he was becoming more curious about girls and seemed to think Kelley held all the answers to his questions about what women wanted or liked. One time she hadn't been home two days, and he had virtually monopolized her time. She was so patient with him, but his incessant demands were beginning to wear on me. So one night I told him we needed a little adult time alone. I have no clue what he thought that meant, but I was so frustrated by then that I didn't care.

"I planned a perfect, intimate evening, complete with candles and soft music. I changed into my nightgown. You know, the kind with the little spaghetti straps, and applied just the right amount of Kelley's favorite perfume in all her favorite places." Sarah's eyes closed and her hand came up against her chest at the sweet memory. "A few minutes later Kelley walked into the bedroom and saw me standing there. She closed and locked the bedroom door before walking toward me. That cute little lop-sided grin that always drove me crazy appeared and, I swear to God, those beautiful brown eyes melted as she looked at me. She leaned down to kiss me. I felt her fingers on my shoulders and the next thing I knew my nightgown was in a puddle on the floor, leaving me totally naked. It was so romantic and perfect, and I wanted her so much." The expression on Sarah's face changed. "Right up until Carl knocked at the bedroom door."

Pauline's hand flew to her mouth and her eyes widened as she broke into laughter.

"Anyway," Sarah continued, "I was so angry that he had interrupted that most excruciatingly passionate moment that I marched my naked self to the door and flung it open. When he saw me standing there, demanding to know what the hell he wanted, he slammed his eyes closed, turned around, and walked away without another word. Kelley was sitting on the edge of our bed laughing so hard that tears came to her eyes. Needless to say, Carl didn't return that night or any other night when I told him Kelley and I needed a little time alone. I can only hope the sight of his mother's naked body didn't traumatize him for life."

Between laughs, Pauline said, "I don't have any stories nearly as entertaining."

"Thank your lucky stars for that," Sarah said, rolling her eyes.

"I had a friend many years ago," Pauline said. "Well, she is still my friend, but she developed an annoying habit of calling at the worst imaginable times. Every time Kelley and I became...intimate, Jolie would call. It was as if she had some kind of sixth sense about it. It annoyed me, certainly, but Kelley was fast developing a dislike for Jolie and telephones. Kelley arrived in town one time, and no sooner were we in bed, aching for one another, than the phone rang. I told Kelley to ignore it, but after about the tenth ring she couldn't any longer. She reached across me to grab the receiver, and I couldn't keep my hands off her. She set the receiver down on the nightstand and kissed me like she never had before. I am certain some thrashing of bedcovers and moaning and groaning was involved. Eventually, we came up for air and Kelley picked up the phone again. She said, 'I'm sorry, Jolie, but I am making love to my wife. Can Pauline call you back when we're done? Say in a couple of days.' Then she hung up." Pauline knitted her eyebrows in thought for a moment. "I don't think I ever did call Jolie back," she laughed.

Sarah slid down farther into the floor pillow beneath her and readjusted her body to rest her head against the cushions of the love seat behind her. She closed her eyes and Pauline watched as a dreamy expression came across Sarah's face. The light from the dying flames in the fireplace illuminated her delicate facial features.

"Thinking about Kelley?" Pauline asked softly.

"No," Sarah answered. "I'm thinking how comfortable I'm feeling right now. A good meal, good wine, good company. It's been a long time since I felt this relaxed and contented."

"I will be sad to leave tomorrow," Pauline murmured into the fire. "But I need to get back to see to my business. Suzanne is a good worker, but certainly doesn't know everything." Pauline downed the last of her wine and pushed against the chair behind her. As she started to rise the chair slid backwards and she lost her balance, falling onto her ass. She stayed there, laughing, for a few minutes. "Remind me not to drink two bottles of wine and then attempt to stand quickly," she laughed. She looked up to see Sarah on her hands and knees beside her.

"Are you all right?" Sarah asked with an amused look.

"Yes. Nothing is hurt except my pride at not being able to hold my wine better than this."

Sarah sat back on her feet and held a hand out to pull her guest up. Pauline took it gratefully and sat up, finding herself no more than a few inches from Sarah's face. As their breath intermingled Pauline brought her hand up to caress Sarah's cheek before slipping it to the back of Sarah's neck. "Do you know how beautiful you are?" she whispered as her lips touched Sarah's. When the response came, Pauline was eager to give what the kiss was demanding. She pulled Sarah closer and took her mouth hungrily, needing to feel a connection to the lovely blonde now resting in her arms. As their kisses became more demanding, Pauline broke her lips away from Sarah's and clutched her desperately in her arms. "This is insane," she whispered.

"I never knew insanity could feel so...so wonderful," Sarah whispered back. "Make me feel again, Pauline. Please," she murmured as she buried her face against Pauline's neck.

Pauline lifted her head to look in Sarah's eyes again. "Are you sure you want this?" she asked.

Sarah hesitated. "Don't you?"

Pauline kissed Sarah tenderly before standing and pulling her up into her arms. She held Sarah's hand and led her down the hallway toward the guest room, pausing along the way to press Sarah against the wall to steal another delicious kiss. Inside Pauline's room, Sarah began to unbutton her blouse. A hand reached out, the fingertips brushing against newly exposed skin above Sarah's lacy flesh-tone bra. "Don't," Pauline rasped. "Please."

Sarah searched Pauline's pleading eyes. She felt the coolness on her skin as Pauline's hand dropped away.

"I'm sorry, Sarah. I can't do this."

Sarah bowed her head and placed her forehead against Pauline chest. "I want to feel whole again." Tears filled her eyes when she looked up and asked, "Is that so wrong?"

"Of course not," Pauline shook her head. "But who would we be making love with? One another or a ghost?" She wrapped her arms around Sarah and held her in a long embrace.

THE DRIVE BACK into Boston seemed longer than usual for Sarah. The silence between the two women added to the length of the trip. Their limited conversation was subdued and uncomfortable. Pauline had been so easy to talk to just the evening before, but now Sarah was embarrassed by the disaster that had almost happened in the guest bedroom. She knew it would have been even worse if Pauline had taken her to bed. Everything would have been even more awkward between them the following morning as they packed to return to the city. What could either of them have said to assuage the other's guilt? It had to have been the wine, Sarah thought. She never drank much because it always lowered her inhibitions to the point of recklessness. Kelley had kidded her about her low tolerance for alcohol before, but assured her she was unbelievably adorable when she was a little tipsy.

Sarah leaned her elbow on the window frame of the Murano

and ran her fingers absently through her hair. She looked across the car seat at Pauline. She was resting her head against the headrest, and Sarah couldn't tell if she was asleep or not. Her sunglasses hid her eyes and her chest rose and fell in a regular, steady breathing pattern. Perhaps Pauline hadn't been able to sleep the night before either.

PAULINE KNEW SARAH was looking at her. She wondered what the attractive blonde must be thinking. How could she have been so callous and stupid as to kiss her? Only three weeks ago her life had been everything she possibly could have wanted. Then her world ended, only to be revived by being near a constant reminder of her loss. *Damn you, Kelley,* she thought bitterly. *Sarah is a wonderful woman. She loved you without reservation, and yet you decided to share half your life with me. What did you think would happen when you were gone? That we would never know or find out about your two lives? You left us both well provided for in every aspect of our lives, except one.*

Pauline watched Sarah comb her fingers through her hair and let it slowly fall away from her fingers. Sarah had lovely, soft hair. It would have been simple to take Sarah to bed the night before, but Pauline would have no respect for herself if she had. Sarah had died a little inside when she lost Kelley, as had she. Pauline wasn't sure she wanted to start her life over again at fifty-five. No one could replace Kelley in her heart and soul. She would continue running her business and put the future out of her mind. She would leave and never see Sarah again. It would be enough. Anything more would be wrong.

SARAH PULLED TO a stop in front of the Air Canada terminal and pressed a button to open the back hatch. Pauline stepped out of the car and took her suitcase from the rear compartment. Sarah joined her as she stood in the short curbside line to check in her baggage.

"You don't have to come in with me," Pauline said without looking at Sarah. "We should say goodbye here."

"Well, have a safe flight home. Did you remember your book?"

Pauline held the book up and finally gave Sarah a smile she wasn't feeling. "I never go anywhere without one."

Sarah looked around awkwardly, searching for something else to say to make their parting more pleasant. Pauline lifted the suitcase onto the scale in front of the terminal and took the claim check from the sky cap.

"I guess I'd better find my gate," Pauline said. She followed Sarah to the driver's side of the car and opened the door for her. "Thank you for sharing your farewell with me," Pauline said. "Now the circle is complete."

Sarah laughed, but it held no humor. "I almost shared a hell of a lot more with you. Remind me someday never to drink that much wine."

Without thinking, Pauline pulled Sarah into a fierce hug and whispered, "I'm so sorry, Sarah." Before Sarah could say anything in return Pauline released her and walked quickly toward the terminal entrance. An airport police officer blew his whistle signaling Sarah to leave the curbside area as she watched Pauline stride through the automatic doors and out of sight.

"You'll have to move along, lady," the officer called out.

Sarah waved toward him and settled into the car. A few minutes later she merged into traffic near the airport and guided her car toward her empty brownstone and her empty future.

Chapter Eight

PAULINE HOISTED HER carry-on bag onto her shoulder and pulled her small forest green, soft-side travel bag behind her. She looked up and down the street running in front of the terminal at the Vancouver airport and didn't see Jolie Marchand's car. She glanced at her wristwatch and walked toward a concrete bench that sat under the canopy between the entrances to the airport. She hunched her shoulders slightly and flipped up the collar of her coat. A brisk October breeze blew constantly down the tunnel created by cars as they loaded and unloaded passengers.

It had been a mistake to accept Sarah's invitation to be with her when she spread Kelley's ashes. She tried in vain to place everything that had happened the last three days in some kind of perspective. She had left the friendly relationship between her and Sarah strained at the least. She hadn't meant for anything to happen, and other than sharing a soul shaking kiss, nothing had happened. Sarah was a wonderful woman whose heart had been shattered. She didn't need Pauline doing anything stupid to make her healing more difficult. But, in a strange way, it had felt good to hold a woman who knew what it was like to be held by the same woman who had held her. Her convoluted thoughts left her feeling a little dizzy, and she shook her head to discard them.

The sound of a car horn brought Pauline thankfully from her thoughts. She waved when she saw Jolie getting out of her vehicle to open the trunk. Pauline took a deep, cleansing breath. Fall would be soon settle over the city and the gray skies would match her mood.

Jolie hugged Pauline and kissed her lightly on the cheek to welcome her home before they went to their separate sides of the car and pulled away.

"Did you enjoy your visit to the States?" Jolie asked.

"It was nice," Pauline said with a nod. "It was pretty with all the leaves changing colors."

Jolie piloted her car toward the heart of the city without much conversation. "Is there anything you need to talk about?" she finally asked.

"No. I'm just tired. It will take me a while to adjust to being alone."

"Then I'll have to make sure you get back out there and mingle."

"I think I need to spend some time alone, Jolie."

"Kelley wouldn't be happy if you shut yourself up in that store and your apartment."

"Oh, and you're such an expert on what made Kelley happy," Pauline snorted.

"I know she'd want you to live a happy life. You can't do that without being around other people. There's a dance next Friday night. Come with me. We'll have a few laughs."

"And probably more than a few drinks, if I know you. Are you ever going to settle down?"

"You did and look where it got you, girlfriend. Besides, I haven't met the right woman yet. Maybe Friday night will be some woman's lucky night. Wouldn't you love to see that?"

Jolie Marchand was an attractive and outgoing woman of forty-eight who had spent most of her life looking for a woman who could make her stop looking at other women. Pauline had been beside her on several occasions when Jolie was trying to find the correct, least hurtful, way to let her conquest of the moment know she no longer found her enticing enough.

"I will go with you, but I want to get home at a decent hour," Pauline said.

"Home by midnight. I promise," Jolie said with a wink. "Unless you get lucky."

"I'm not looking for anyone, Jolie. I need time to think about what's happened and find a way to accept it. It's very doubtful I'd find anyone in a bar. Everyone there is so young. They're not interested in a woman my age. I gave up one-night stands in my twenties."

"You found Marie in a bar."

"And look where that got me. A semi-private room in a hospital. That alone should be a good enough reason to avoid picking up a woman in a bar. Learn from my mistake, Jolie."

"You were a kid then. You're smarter now and know what love is. You're one of the lucky ones. I've slept with many women over the years, but have never known love."

"You will," Pauline said. "It's never too late to find love. It sounds like you're still confusing love with sex."

"Nothing wrong with good sex."

"No, there isn't. It's an important part of any relationship, but not the only part." Pauline gazed out the front window. "It's...it's being able to spend time alone together and doing nothing terribly important. Maybe reading, cross stitch, playing cards, anything. Then you look into the other person's eyes and see her looking at you, her eyes filled with the love, caring, and desire she feels for you. It's something very special and worth looking for. It's so easy to say I love you. You expect to say it and hear it when you're making love without knowing if either of you means it. But what you see in her eyes can't be a lie. It's everything."

"I never realized you were such a romantic."

"Neither did I until I knew what love really was."

"What if you found someone you really loved, but they don't feel the same? She could see it in your eyes if she looked, but it wasn't returned in hers."

"That would be heartbreaking and one of you would be hurt."

"Is that what happened with you and Marie?"

Pauline shook her head firmly. "Marie wanted only my body. She never loved me. How I felt wasn't of any concern to her as long as she was satisfied. I think I knew that, but like a fool I continued going back to her over and over."

"When do you just settle? You know, get tired of trolling and accept someone who cares for you more than you care for them. So you won't be alone when you get older."

"Never. It is better to be alone than to pretend to love another."

Pauline closed her eyes and thought of how close she'd come with Sarah. She was a lovely woman faced with being alone for the first time in a very long time. Sarah and Pauline shared a common loneliness. They'd both lost the source of their happiness. Perhaps that was why Pauline had been so tempted to succumb to Sarah's need for intimacy. But more than intimacy, they both needed time to heal.

After Jolie dropped her off at the bookstore, Pauline quickly unpacked her small suitcase and fixed a sandwich. Traveling always seemed to leave her tired and she decided to retire early that evening. She took a quick shower and wrapped her robe snugly around her body. She was just turning the bedcovers down when the telephone in the front room began ringing. It was only nine o'clock and Pauline was sure it would be Jolie.

"*Qui*, my stubborn friend," she said when she picked up the receiver. "I only saw you two hours ago and it wasn't enough for one evening?"

"Pauline?" a voice questioned.

The voice was female and crackled through the static on the line. "This is Pauline Champion. Can I help you?" she asked.

"I didn't mean to disturb you, but I wanted to know you got home safely."

"Sarah?"

"Yes."

Pauline glanced at the clock on her mantle. "It must be at least midnight there."

"I couldn't sleep. I didn't mean to disturb you."

"You didn't. Are you all right? You sound tired." Pauline carried the handset to the sofa and curled her feet beneath her to get comfortable.

"I'm fine." Sarah paused for a moment, making Pauline wonder if she had hung up.

"Sarah?"

"I'm sorry, Pauline. I shouldn't have called. I'm glad you survived your trip and, well, I wanted to thank you again for being here. I'm sorry I had too much to drink and made such a fool out of myself. I can only imagine what you must be thinking about me and I don't blame you. I–"

"Sarah, don't do this to yourself. Please. You didn't do anything wrong."

Pauline heard the sadness in Sarah's voice and heard her sniff before speaking again. "I hope you'll forget the entire incident. It wasn't like me to behave like that with someone who is practically a total stranger."

"It's forgotten."

"Thank you. That's all I really wanted to say, so I guess this is goodbye."

"I wish we could have met under different circumstances, Sarah."

"So do I."

Pauline set the wireless handset down carefully. She hoped Sarah would be all right once the shock of Kelley's death and the revelation of her betrayal had had time to fade. Pauline ran her hands through her hair. She had come so close, too close, to losing her senses when she kissed and held Sarah in her arms. It would have been so easy to use Sarah to console her own grief, but Pauline still had to face herself in the mirror every day. She knew she wouldn't have liked the reflection looking back at her if she had taken Sarah to bed.

PAULINE LEFT THE bookstore in the capable hands of Suzanne for the remainder of the week after she returned to Vancouver. She needed time alone to think about her life. She drove back to the cliffs where she and Sarah had scattered Kelley's ashes and sat on a blanket gazing out at the ocean. Sometimes she spoke aloud, hoping Kelley could hear her and tell her what to do. Suddenly, she didn't have to worry about money or owning a home. According to Kelley's will, Pauline was now the sole owner of the building where the store and her apartment were located. When she returned home, the title to the property was in the stack of mail waiting for her. She had never worried about money, even when Kelley was alive. They lived a comfortable life with few worries. Despite that, Pauline felt strangely unsettled and she realized it was because she no longer had someone to share her life with. When Kelley was with her, she had loved telling Kelley everything of interest that had happened during her days. She loved hearing what her lover's day had been like. The low soft sound of Kelley's voice brought a peaceful end to their days.

Pauline rested on her blanket and watched the clouds skim through the blue sky above her. Perhaps she was a dreamer, as Kelley had accused her of being many times. Now that she had no problems to occupy her time, what were her dreams? Perhaps she would return to what she had given up when she met Kelley.

PAULINE CHECKED HER appearance in the bedroom mirror before she walked through the living room to open the apartment door.

A low wolf whistle greeted her. "You look great!" Jolie said. Pauline was wearing casual clothes, jeans, and the pullover top Jolie had always liked. The pullover had a wide neckline that let it slip down and reveal a partial shoulder. She wore comfortable shoes. "*Merci.* You look good, too," Pauline said. "Come in. I'll be ready in a minute."

Jolie looked around the apartment. "You've made a few changes," she observed.

"I don't need things to remind me of Kelley," Pauline said quietly.

"What do you have going on in the corner?"

"I've been doing a little writing," Pauline shrugged.

"You're going to start writing again?"

"Perhaps. Are you ready?"

After a light dinner, Jolie escorted Pauline into a women's dance club and scanned the room for friends. She spotted a large semi-circular booth near the back and pointed to it. One of the women seated in the booth half stood and waved to them. When Pauline and Jolie joined the four other women, they spent the next half an hour getting acquainted. All of them were older professional women who enjoyed having a good time, and Pauline felt at home with them. She was halfway through a glass of wine when Jolie grabbed her hand and pulled her away from the booth.

"It looks like we're dancing," she laughed with a shrug. The other women followed close behind and joined Jolie and Pauline on the dance floor. Pauline enjoyed the freedom dancing gave her, but she hadn't danced in quite a long time. However, it didn't take her long to fall into a rhythm that matched the music. The song was a medium beat, and her legs told her she would be sore the next morning. She was grateful when the beat of the music slowed down considerably and accepted a dance with one of Jolie's friends, an attractive office manager for a Vancouver law firm.

"I'm glad you could join us tonight," the woman, Lizette, said. "Jolie told us you recently lost your wife. I am sorry."

"Thank you," Pauline said. "It is hard suddenly being alone."

"You've got good friends. You won't be alone. Don't be afraid to go out. You won't be breaking anyone's trust."

The evening went by quickly and several rounds of drinks were consumed by all the women. Jolie looked at her wristwatch and tapped Pauline on the shoulder.

"We'd better go if I want to get you home before you turn into a pumpkin," she said.

"We can stay a little longer. I'm having a good time and it feels good to laugh and enjoy good company," Pauline said.

"Then let's have another dance," Jolie said.

Pauline felt relaxed for the first time since Kelley's death. The music was slow and romantic and seemed to wash over her. When Jolie took her into her arms Pauline realized what Sarah had felt at the cabin. It was a sudden overwhelming need to be comforted, the desire to be with someone, anyone, who might make her feel again. She brought her arms up and rested them on Jolie's shoulders, looking deeply into her eyes. Slowly her arms encircled her friend's neck and drew her into a heated kiss. Jolie stopped dancing and responded to the touch of Pauline's lips on hers.

"I'm ready to go home now," Pauline whispered when their lips parted.

Jolie could only nod as she quietly escorted Pauline toward the table when the music ended. The drive back to Pauline's building was silent. Pauline rested her head on the headrest of the passenger seat and watched the red, yellow, white, and blue signs of various businesses flash by. A light rain had started and the lights of the city created a colorful Jackson Pollock abstract painting on the black pavement.

In the late hour Jolie easily found a parking space close to the bookstore. She walked around her vehicle and opened the passenger door, then followed Pauline through the store and up the stairs to her apartment.

Pauline went into her bedroom. Jolie walked up behind her and kissed the back of her neck, her hands resting on Pauline's hips. Pauline covered Jolie's hands with her own and guided them around her waist and up to her breasts. She could feel the heat from Jolie's body increase.

"Do you know how long I've dreamed of being with you?" Jolie asked softly. "But you never gave me a second look."

Pauline turned to face Jolie. "I'm looking now." Her voice was seductive and Jolie swallowed hard, unable to tear her eyes away from Pauline's.

Pauline took Jolie's face in her hands and kissed her softly. She pulled away a step and tugged the pullover over her head, dropping it on the floor. "I need you, Jolie," she said in a husky voice filled with emotion.

"Since the first day we met I've dreamed of making love to you. Longed to feel your nipples tighten in my mouth. I thought if I only waited long enough I would have a chance. But then you met Kelley and my chance had slipped through my fingers," Jolie replied.

"Kelley is gone," Pauline said softly.

Jolie shook her head. "She's still here. Her spirit is so thick in the air I can almost reach out and touch her. I know you feel her presence too. As much as I want you, Pauline, I can't. I can't be Kelley."

Pauline leaned her head back and closed her eyes as she brought a hand up to Jolie's chest. "I'm sorry, Jolie," she said softly.

"I feel like an idiot."

Pauline stroked the side of Jolie's face. "Don't. I should never have put you in this position."

"I love you, so much," Jolie said, turning her head slightly to kiss Pauline's palm.

"I love you, too."

"But not in the way that counts. I know that. I've always known that. You could never look at me the way you looked at Kelley."

"I'm sorry, Jolie." Pauline bent down and picked up her pullover, drawing it over her head.

"I'll always be your friend, Pauline. Maybe one day Kelley's memory will begin to fade, and you will want new memories to replace them."

Pauline stepped closer and took Jolie into her arms. "I understand more than you'll ever know," Pauline said, thinking back to the night Sarah had wanted her to make love to her. Now she understood what Sarah felt and why. Obviously Jolie wanted her, but refused to take advantage of her. Pauline had refused to use Sarah's weakness against her as well. Pauline had wanted to make love with Sarah, and the realization strangely saddened her.

Chapter Nine

CHERISH HAWTHORNE STAMPED snow from her feet on the covered porch of the two-story brick house in Cambridge and rang the doorbell. She looked at the heavy metal gray sky and cursed the thought of more snow that was predicted for later that afternoon. She prayed it waited until after she picked Ethan up from school. Her attention returned to the door as it swung open a few minutes later. Carl stood in the entry, his hand holding a towel that was wrapped loosely around his waist.

"That's an interesting fashion statement," she said as she stepped past him. "The hair's a nice touch, too."

"Have you ever heard of a telephone?" he smirked.

"Have you ever considered answering the damn thing?" she snapped.

Cherish looked around the downstairs at stacks of boxes and laughed at the sight of a trail of clothing leading from the living room and up the stairs. She patted him on the shoulder and removed her jacket. "Sorry if my timing sucks. I was a newlywed myself once."

"Make yourself comfortable, Sis. I'll get Angela and we'll be down in a minute," Carl said over his shoulder as he picked up underwear and other garments on his way upstairs.

Cherish wandered through the house and into the kitchen. She searched through boxes and cabinets until she found the coffee and coffeemaker. She prepared the pot and leaned against the counter, waiting for the machine to burp out the hot liquid.

"Sorry the house is such a mess," Cherish's sister-in-law said as she strolled into the kitchen. Angela was the only woman Cherish knew who actually looked sexy in baggy jeans, a flannel shirt, and flip flops.

Cherish liked Angela and thought Carl was a lucky man to find such a beautiful woman to share his life with. Angela's long hair was piled loosely on top of her head and her olive skin glowed.

"I tried calling before dropping in, Ange, but no one answered the home phone and Carl's cell went to voicemail."

"Not a problem. You're welcome here any time," Angela said as she took three mugs from a cabinet next to the sink and set them on the counter.

"In fact, why don't you stay awhile and unpack some boxes with us," Carl said as he walked into the kitchen. He greeted

Angela with a quick kiss and picked up a mug.

"Pass," Cherish said as she poured coffee into the three mugs. "Been there, done that. Cute house, by the way."

"It's big enough for us," Carl shrugged. "It's close to work for both of us and the payments were right. So, what's up?"

"We need to talk about Mom," Cherish said.

"I'll clear a place to sit in the front room," Angela said.

"Is something wrong with Mom?" Carl asked when they were all situated.

"Have you talked to her lately?" Cherish asked.

"I called her yesterday. Angela and I took off this week to get the house in shape. We thought we'd take her out to dinner one night."

"Good luck with that," Cherish said. "Since Christmas she's locked herself in her house like a fricking shut-in. Nathan and I have invited her over several times, but she always makes up some lame ass excuse. I'm worried about her."

"She's still getting over losing Kelley," Carl shrugged. "It'll take time."

"It's been four months, Carl. She was only going through the motions at Thanksgiving and Christmas. She hasn't been anywhere or done anything. Kelley's dead, but Mom's still alive. She needs to start living again."

"I agree, but it's hard when you're surrounded by things that remind you of the person you lost," Carl said. "I go to work at Bilt-Rite every day, but I can't make a decision without thinking about what Kelley would do. It's getting easier, but it will always be there. And I didn't love her the way Mom did."

"That's my point, Carl. Mom has to find a way to let what she felt for Kelley become a pleasant memory and not her whole life. She's only fifty-three years old, for God's sake. She needs to get out and socialize."

"You expect Mom to find a new girlfriend?"

"No. Now that she's out from under Kelley, no pun intended, she needs to find a man to take care of her."

"Listen to yourself, Cherish," Carl said. "Mom's not looking for a man. She's a lesbian!"

"She's confused," Cherish said adamantly.

"And you're delusional," Carl laughed. "The only time Mom was confused was when she married our father, the jerk!"

"Shut up, Carl!"

"Look, Sis, Mom's not looking for anyone, male or female. Let her finish her grieving process. Let her work it out. She and Kelley were together a damn long time. She won't get over her loss for a while."

Their conversation was interrupted by the ring of the house phone. Angela excused herself and left the room to answer it. A few minutes later she walked back into the living room and plopped on the couch next to Carl.

"Everyone get your coats," Angela said. She looked at Carl. "That was Sarah. I told her Cherish was here. She wants us all to come to her house."

SARAH OPENED THE front door of the Back Bay brownstone and ushered her children and daughter-in-law inside. Cherish unzipped her ski jacket and pulled it off. She opened the entry closet and took out a hanger. As she hung the coat inside she asked, "Have you gotten rid of some of your coats? This closet is practically empty," she said as she hung her jacket up and took Carl and Angela's.

Sarah walked into the front room of her home and poked absently at the fire she had started that morning. "I've taken Kelley's coats and jackets out and packed them away," she said when they had all joined her. "I've made a few decisions I think you should be aware of."

Cherish glanced at Carl and said, "What's up, Mom?"

"I've decided to sell the cabin in Vermont," Sarah said. "I've already contacted a realtor." She looked around the front room. "And I'll be placing the brownstone on the market in the spring. That gives me two or three months to go through everything and make the repairs she suggested."

"But this home and the cabin have been in Kelley's family for nearly a hundred years," Carl said as he sat down.

"Kelley has no remaining family except us," Sarah said. "That's why I called you all over here." Sarah cleared her throat and spoke again. "Cherish, I know Nathan has always admired the desk and barrister bookcases in Kelley's office. I thought perhaps he might like to have them for his office."

"I'm sure he would love them. I'll ask him and let you know."

"Carl, you and Angela have a new home. If there's anything you'd like, please feel free to take it. I'm keeping only a few things that meant something personally to Kelley and me together. Everything else can go."

"Most of the furniture is antique," Cherish said.

"Which is just another word for old furniture," Sarah said. "As for the brownstone itself," she sighed. "It was too big for the two of us after you and Carl moved out. The maintenance alone is a small fortune. We were already discussing selling it. In return, I need your help. The basement is a complete disaster. I seriously doubt there's anything of much worth gathering dust down there, but I can't move some of the boxes by myself. Somewhere in that mess are a few old photo albums I'd like to look through and keep, but otherwise everything else can go."

Cherish paused before asking her next question, uncertain how Sarah would react. "Why now?

"I don't need 'things' to remind me of Kelley," Sarah said softly. "Personal possessions don't make a person. Memories do." As much as she hated not being able to control her emotions, Sarah could feel tears beginning to form in her eyes. "Kelley will always live here," Sarah managed, patting her chest. "In my heart."

"I don't understand why you're suddenly stripping everything from your life. The cabin, Kelley's personal belongings. Maybe even this house."

"Kelley's dead," Sarah snapped, her voice hard. "Hanging on to the cabin or this house won't bring her back," she continued. "The cabin was meant to be enjoyed, and I've decided someone else should have the chance to get as much happiness from it as we have."

"For the last four months you've clung to Kelley's memory like your life depended on it," Cherish said. "Now you're getting rid of everything that reminds you of her. Is this your way of punishing Kelley because she loved another woman?"

Sarah turned toward her daughter quickly, her hands clenched into fists at her sides. "Why would you give a shit!" she said loudly. "I thought you, of all people, would be thrilled to see every last possible hint that Kelley ever existed gone!"

"You're twenty-five years too late!" Cherish yelled back. "She took you away from us, and you didn't do a damn thing about it. You chose her over us."

"I've always been here for you and Carl," Sarah said. "Didn't I deserve to be happy?"

Cherish cast a glance in Carl's direction. "Being with us wasn't enough to make you happy, I suppose."

"I was a grown woman, for Christ's sake! I needed someone in my bed. Someone to hold me and tell me everything was going to be fine. To tell me *I* mattered."

"If you had known Kelley was sleeping with that other woman would you have kicked her ass out the way you did our father?"

"But I didn't know. Am I mad at her? I've never been so mad or felt so betrayed, but there's nothing I can do about it now." Sarah stepped closer and pulled Cherish into her arms. "I never meant to cause either of you so much pain," she whispered as Cherish clung tightly against her. She took Cherish's face in her hands and met her eyes. "You and Carl are grown. Now I need to take care of myself the best way I can. That will never mean I love either of you less." She held her arm out toward Carl.

When he joined them for a family hug he said, "There's a new doctor on Angela's service at the hospital, Mom. And let me tell ya, she's pretty freakin' hot. And single."

Sarah looked at him as she kissed the top of Cherish's head. "Really, dear? Did you get her telephone number?" she asked with a soft laugh.

Chapter Ten

BY LATE MARCH Sarah sat in Walter's office reading over the provisions for the sale of the cabin in Vermont. In deference to what she knew would be Kelley's wishes, the cabin and the acreage surrounding it could only be sold as a single unit and the property never divided to allow construction of additional homes. It would remain isolated the way Kelley wanted it to be. She made a trip to Vermont to pick up a few personal items she wanted to keep. It didn't amount to more than two medium-sized cardboard boxes, mostly pictures and trinkets they had discovered on trips. She left the remainder of the furniture with the cabin. If the new owner didn't wish to keep the current furnishings they would have no trouble selling them off and replacing them.

That evening she prepared a simple dinner, setting two places at the table, as she always had, and ate a final dinner accompanied by only her memories. She gazed across the table at the empty chair and let the memories come back to her. It had been six months since the world had spun off its axis, leaving her alone to regain her equilibrium. *Why? Why did you leave me, darling? Why did you leave me with this ache, these doubts? Why wasn't I enough? I gave you everything. I belonged to you and no one else. I thought you belonged to me alone. How could I have been so wrong? Was I nothing but a fool?*

Sarah's thoughts ate at her. She should have had been soothed by her memories of Kelley. Remembering her touch, her kisses, should have offered some comfort. Lingering behind the memories of being in Kelley's arms were the unbidden pictures of Kelley holding Pauline. Sarah frowned as she saw herself replaced by the other Mrs. Champion. It was Pauline's face she saw bathed in ecstasy as Kelley stroked her body and caressed her. Sarah shook her head to throw off the picture in her mind. She replaced it with the memory of Pauline's hands touching her. She saw Pauline's face, smiling as her lips met Sarah's. She was startled when the remembrance of Pauline's lips on hers made her abdomen clench with desire. The desire she saw in Pauline's eyes as she looked into Sarah's eyes, only to be rejected, crashed down on her and she shoved away from the table.

Kelley no longer needed her. She was dead. There was nothing more forever than that. Pauline had left her humiliated and unfulfilled. She was truly alone now. She could no longer live with only the memories that had once sustained her. They were tainted with new and unwelcome ones. She cleaned the dishes from dinner and scanned the living room. This had once been an important part of her life, but now she knew it had all been a lie.

She rose before dawn after spending the night in the cabin and loaded the car. She closed the door to the cabin gently and allowed her hand to rest on the door frame for a few moments before she got into her car and pulled away.

An hour later Sarah brushed snow from the flat boulder on Mt. Mansfield and waited to say good morning as the warmth of the sunlight caressed her face in a return greeting. "Tell me what to do, sweetheart," she said to no one but herself as warmth spread slowly throughout her body. "Tell me you won't be disappointed in me." She opened her eyes and tilted her head back, inhaling the fresh morning air that was so different from the air in the city. It was clean, fresh, and pure. In the distance, gray-white clouds floated across the sky. The piercing cry of a falcon soaring high above drew her attention as it circled lazily, catching updrafts from the mountains. The bird seemed to hover over where she was lying before shifting its wings and banking away toward the west, chasing the sun.

SARAH LOOKED AT herself in the beveled, full-length mirror in her bedroom. She made a full three-sixty to make sure everything was in place before making her way down the staircase to the ground floor. Even though she had finally completed the renovations to the interior of the brownstone, everywhere she looked she saw a reminder of Kelley. The couch they picked out together, a painting Kelley gave Sarah as a birthday present, the crown molding Kelley had insisted on installing herself. Kelley was everywhere around her and while the memories were sweet, they still brought back the lingering grief. Alone at night in the cavernous home, Sarah seemed to be waiting for the sound of Kelley's footsteps making their way up the staircase toward the room where Sarah waited.

Sarah shook her head to drive the thoughts from her mind and pulled her best coat from the entry closet. She was too alone and knew it. She had never dreamed of the day when she would be so alone. She and Kelley had planned future vacations, talked about retirement, looked through brochures for a trip one day to the Greek Isles. They had talked about everything. Everything except being alone. She wondered what Kelley would have done if left alone suddenly. What a stupid thought. Kelley would still have had Pauline to fill her nights. Sarah was relieved when the doorbell in the hallway chimed its melodic tones.

CARL TOOK BOTH Sarah and Angela's wraps and left them with a young woman in the coat room of the Westin Hotel. Sarah followed Carl and Angela down the plush carpeting toward the sound of music coming from the ballroom. Angela wore an elegant burgundy gown accented by an empire waistline. Her long blonde hair fell gracefully over her shoulders with the center pulled back and held in place by a comb. Carl was the picture of a proud husband in his new tuxedo and quickly found seats for them at a table far enough away from the small band providing the music to make conversation possible. As soon as Sarah was seated, Carl pulled Angela toward the dance floor. A waiter in black pants and a white waistcoat stopped to offer Sarah a flute of champagne, which she took gratefully. She watched Carl and Angela dance, dredging up memories of all the times she and Kelley had danced together. Would she ever be able to go someplace and not think of a time she and Kelley had shared? She stared blankly at the glass in her hand.

"Excuse me," a pleasantly low-timbered voice said.

Sarah raised her head and looked into the equally pleasant face of a tall woman with short, stylish silver hair that swept rakishly across her forehead. Sarah scanned the woman from head to waist. She looked incredibly elegant in the tuxedo jacket over a dark paisley vest that seemed to shimmer in the dim lighting provided by the ballroom chandeliers. Her metallic-framed glasses blended well with her hair, but Sarah wasn't able to determine the woman's eye color.

"I couldn't help but notice when you came in with Angela and her husband." Reaching across the large round table the woman extended her hand. "I'm Emma Rodgers. I work with Angela. May I join you?" she asked, indicating an empty chair next to Sarah.

"I'm sorry," Sarah said. "My mind was obviously elsewhere. Please have a seat."

Emma unbuttoned her jacket and sat down. "Is the champagne any good?' she asked.

"I suppose. A waiter handed it to me. He's probably running around nearby if you'd like a glass."

Emma rested her elbows on the table. "I'm not much of a champagne drinker. I personally prefer something a little...meatier," she said with a wink. She was temporarily distracted by a passing waiter and stopped him to place an order. "A brandy for me," she told him. "Would you care for one?" she asked Sarah. "Make that two," she amended after Sarah's nod.

The music stopped and Carl escorted Angela back to their table.

"Dr. Rodgers," Angela said. "It's nice to see you again."

Emma laughed. "Yeah, it's been a long time. Probably a whole two hours since we last saw one another."

"I see you've already met my mother-in-law."

"Sort of, although she hasn't yet graced me with her name. We've been discussing the attributes of various alcoholic beverages."

"Mom doesn't drink much," Carl volunteered.

"Is that right, Mom?" Emma asked, turning her head to look at Sarah.

"Sarah. Sarah Champion," Sarah finally said, offering her hand.

"A lovely name, my dear."

"Dr. Rodgers is the new attending physician on my service," Angela said.

"And Angela is one of my best young doctors," Emma said.

"Sounds like a mutual admiration society," Sarah smirked.

"It's a nasty job, but someone has to do it," Emma said with a charming grin. "Would you care to dance?" she asked when the band started a slower tune. "I don't think we'll throw any body parts out of whack with this one." She stood and held a hand out toward Sarah.

"Go on, Mom. You love to dance," Carl encouraged.

Sarah shrugged and accepted Emma's hand, allowing herself to be led into the mass of people already on the dance floor. Emma turned around as soon as she entered the floor and smoothly led off into the rhythm of the music. She didn't hold Sarah too close or at arm's length. They were close enough to carry on a conversation without straining to hear.

"Angela tells me you're a widow," Emma said. "How long ago did you lose your partner?"

"Six months ago."

"It's hard to get back into the business of life, isn't it? I lost mine four years ago and some days it seems like it was only yesterday."

"How long were you together?"

Emma seemed to think for a minute before answering. "As long as I can remember," she said. "Over thirty years, but I'm really bad with dates."

"Did it take you long to accept your loss?"

"You never accept it. You adjust and try to move on, one day at a time."

They danced quietly through the remainder of the dance, but when the band started another slow tune they remained on the floor.

"I meant to tell you that you look lovely in that gown," Emma said. "It really captures your eyes."

"The mirror to the soul, as my wife used to say," Sarah said softly.

"Absolutely," Emma said.

For the first time Sarah noticed the blue-gray of Emma's eyes staring into hers. What she saw reflecting back at her made Sarah feel alive for the first time in months. She felt comfortable in Emma's arms, her sure hand pressing lightly into Sarah's back, guiding her around the floor. Although she was tired and ready to go to bed by the time Carl and Angela dropped her off at the brownstone, Sarah was glad she had gone with them.

"HELLO?" SARAH SAID three days later when she picked up the telephone in the kitchen.

"Sarah. This is Emma Rodgers. I wondered if you'd care to have dinner with me Saturday evening. There's a great seafood place near the docks, if you like seafood."

"The weatherman is forecasting more snow for the weekend. Would you consider a counter offer?"

"Depends on what it is."

"How about a home cooked meal, including drinks, and I'll throw in a warm house and dessert?"

"That sounds like an offer no one in her right mind could turn down."

"Are you considering turning it down?"

"I may be occasionally a little strange, but I'm not crazy. When, and what should I bring?"

"Saturday evening about seven. You don't need to bring a thing."

"Except my charming self?"

"Please leave your other selves at home. You can ask Angela for the address."

Emma laughed and the sound of it made Sarah smile. "I'll see you Saturday," Emma said cheerfully before disconnecting.

Sarah liked Emma Rodgers and their semi-flirtatious conversation made her feel good, a part of the real world again.

The weatherman was right for once. Snow began falling Friday afternoon and was still coming down Saturday. Sarah expected a phone call from Emma to cancel their dinner, but it never came. The chimes in the hallway rang at six-fifty. When Sarah opened the front door, the sight of Emma made her breath catch in her throat. Emma looked even more handsome than she had the previous weekend. Everything about her seemed to be perfect, from her Irish cable knit pullover down to her jeans and boots.

"Sorry I look a little like Nanook of the North," Emma said as she stepped into the entryway.

"You look comfortable," Sarah said.

Emma reached out and touched the soft, velour pantsuit Sarah had chosen for the evening. "This feels comfortable," she said before taking her coat off.

"I thought you might change your mind, considering the snow."

"If my postman can make it on his appointed rounds, I figured I could as well." Emma looked around. "This is a beautiful brownstone."

"Thank you. It's too large for just one person so I'm considering selling it. My realtor tells me it would have a good chance in the spring. So I'm rather stuck here for a few more months. The upkeep on these houses is more than I want to face alone. I've already shut down the top two floors," Sarah explained as they made their way toward the kitchen.

"I bought a loft apartment when I moved here last year," Emma said. "Like you, I didn't need the extra space. I can barely keep up what I have now. Something smells delicious."

"It's nothing special, but sometimes simple foods are the best. And certainly the easiest, so don't think I've been slaving away over a hot stove all day making dinner."

"I'm crushed," Emma said, clutching at her chest to feign injury.

"How are things at the hospital?"

"Okay. Usually I don't talk about work outside of work. Work is work, and my personal time is just that. I try not to mix the two. Especially when I'm with a beautiful woman who's prepared a home cooked meal for me."

"Thank you," Sarah replied. "I'll let you open that bottle of wine on the counter while I get dinner on the table. There's a corkscrew in the drawer beneath it."

It wasn't long before they were seated across from one another and filling their plates.

"I hope it's all right," Sarah said. "As I said, it's nothing fancy."

"That's the best food usually and I love Italian," Emma said as she poured both wine glasses half full. "Tell me about your wife."

Sarah hadn't expected Kelley to be a topic of conversation. "What would you like to know?"

"Whatever you'd like to tell me. Talking about her will make her seem more real to me."

"I think you would have liked Kelley. She was sweet and

unassuming. A nice person who always made you feel you were important. This brownstone belonged to her. It's been in her family since it was first built."

"A stroke, wasn't it?"

"Yes. She was in upper management with the Bilt-Rite Home Centers and traveled a great deal of the time while I stayed home with the children."

"How many children do you have?"

"Two. You already know Carl and I have a daughter, Cherish. They're both married and live in Boston. We have one grandson who's now six. What about your wife?"

"Her name was Melanie. She was the most beautiful woman I'd ever seen. Unfortunately, we never lived in a place that would have recognized our marriage. She lifted me up when I was down and told me off when I occasionally behaved like an egotistical jackass. The first thing she told me about herself was that she hated cooking and cleaning so I'd better earn enough money to hire a housekeeper and enjoy eating out," Emma said. "She was a writer, primarily historical novels. I spent most of my vacations in places she wanted to research, but they were always fun."

Sarah watched Emma's face. Even though she had told Sarah she had lost her partner four years earlier, Sarah could see she still felt the pain of her loss. She wondered if anyone ever got over that feeling of emptiness.

"How did you lose her?" Sarah asked.

"Multiple sclerosis. An insidious disease. As a doctor, I was frustrated that I couldn't do anything for her to alleviate her pain and suffering. Near the end she...she begged me to do something. To end it all."

Sarah reached across the table and covered Emma's hand with her own, squeezing it lightly. "I'm sorry, Emma. I didn't mean to bring up something that obviously brings you such pain."

"I think I would have preferred Melanie to have had a fatal stroke. At least it was over quickly."

Sarah thought about that for a moment. "I couldn't have stood watching Kelley suffer. There were things I would have liked to tell her, but didn't have the chance. She was just...gone."

"I guess when you get right down to it, there is no good way to say good-bye to someone you care so much about," Emma said.

"We should honor them by living well," Sarah said. She took a deep breath. "And by talking about something more pleasant."

"What kind of things do you enjoy doing in your leisure time?" Emma asked.

"I used to do all kinds of things." Sarah rested her chin on her hands and tapped a finger against her lips. "I play golf and some tennis. I read. I used to ski like a maniac once I learned. Now I'm much more cautious. Don't think the bones can handle it like they once did," she said.

"Do you like sailing?"

Sarah cocked her head to one side and said, "I don't know. The only boat I've been on was a cruise ship. You barely realize it's moving." While she had shared a ride on the ferry with Pauline, she decided not to mention it.

"When the weather is better I'll take you out on my sailboat. It's a relaxing way to spend a day, with the wind whipping through your hair and an occasional spray of water on your face."

"And the occasional bout of sea sickness?"

"I recommend Dramamine. Usually you get over it."

"Do you ever see any whales?"

"Occasionally near Martha's Vineyard. It depends on the time of year."

"I love watching whales," Sarah said. "They're so free."

"You'll feel free again one day, Sarah," Emma said softly as she turned her hand over to grasp Sarah's.

"Promise?"

"I promise. It takes a while, but it happens."

"Are you volunteering to be my grief counselor?" Sarah asked.

"I'd like to apply for the position. You deserve to be happy again."

"And you'll make me happy?"

"That depends. Only you know what makes you happy."

"What do you miss most about Melanie?"

Emma leaned back in her chair and thought. "Honestly? The simplest things. Her hand on my arm to draw my attention to something, watching her chew on the eraser of her pencil when she was writing, her almost child-like enthusiasm. Little things. What about you?"

"The way she looked at me when she thought I didn't see her," Sarah said. "Her laugh."

Both women became temporarily lost in their memories before Emma finally broke the silence. "Well, that was a pleasant stroll down memory lane."

Sarah laughed. "I seem to be doing that quite a bit lately."

"Nothing wrong with that. If the weather cooperates, I was wondering if you'd like to have dinner with me next weekend. There's a wonderful seafood restaurant near the harbor."

"I'd love to, Emma. Perhaps you can help me find a new place to live. I've scheduled an appointment with my realtor to look at a few places over the next month or so."

Sarah and Emma spent the remainder of the evening talking.

Sarah felt comfortable with Emma and almost hated to see the evening end.

"Are you sure you'll be able to get home safely?" Sarah asked as she handed Emma her coat a little after ten.

"Slow and steady," Emma said. "I have plenty of gas, the heater works, and there won't be many other vehicles slip-sliding on the road."

"Do you have your cell phone?"

"Yes, mother," Emma kidded.

"I just meant if anything happens, call and I'll get help to you."

Emma brought a hand up to caress Sarah's cheek. "I know. I'm sorry, but I'm not used to having anyone worry about me. I'll give you a call when I get home."

Emma dropped her hand to Sarah's shoulder and searched her face for a moment before brushing her lips against Sarah's softly and pulling away. "Thank you for a lovely evening."

TWO HOURS PASSED before Sarah's phone finally rang. She had cleaned the kitchen and taken a shower before climbing into bed to read and was beginning to doze off. Her eyes snapped open and she picked up the receiver.

"I was beginning to worry about you," she said.

"Did I wake you?" Emma asked.

"No. I was reading before I went to sleep."

"I'm sorry to call so late, but I just got home."

"Did you have much trouble?"

"No. The roads were fine if you know how to drive in this kind of weather. Apparently the guy from Florida ahead of me wasn't familiar with the concept of snow and managed to slide into a ditch. I stopped to help and called a wrecker for him. It took them a while to get there, and I hated to leave him there alone."

"Ah. The Good Samaritan routine, huh?"

"And they say we northeasterners are cold and uncaring."

She listened to the lightness of Emma's voice. "I enjoyed this evening," Sarah said softly. "It's nice to have a friend I can talk to."

"Anytime. I'll try to avoid using that concerned look doctors always seem to have even though I've spent years perfecting it. I need to take a shower to warm up and you need to get a good night's rest. So hang up. Doctor's orders."

"I'll see you next weekend," Sarah said.

"Wouldn't miss it," Emma said before hanging up.

Sarah turned her reading light off and snuggled down under her covers. She liked Emma. She was comfortable to be around and easy to talk to. Sarah hoped they could become good friends. She remembered the touch of Emma's lips against hers and sighed. It hadn't been a passionate kiss, but was pleasant nonetheless. She wondered what Emma's kiss might have been like if driven by desire. Perhaps she would discover that the following weekend.

Chapter Eleven

THE NEXT WEEK flew by as Sarah continued going through the brownstone, taking what she could from the rooms and storing them in two of the downstairs rooms. The weather cleared enough for her to pack the last of Kelley's clothing into her car and deliver them to a second-hand store run by a charitable organization she had donated to in the past.

She met Walter for lunch one day and his partner, Michael, joined them. They hadn't spoken often since their return from Vancouver, and Sarah missed visiting with them. Kelley and Sarah had once entertained at their home regularly, but now it seemed as if she rarely saw any of their friends. Perhaps it was her fault for shutting herself away or perhaps they all simply assumed she needed some time alone. Time alone had become the enemy, and now she needed to be with others.

Emma sent flowers twice during the week and had called simply to chat while she was on a break from seeing patients. By the time Saturday came, Sarah was looking forward to seeing her again. Emma called around noon and announced she was on her way. It was a brisk day and snow was still everywhere, but the sun was shining. It would be a wonderful day for a walk to work up an appetite, Sarah thought.

When the door bell chimed, Sarah opened the door dressed in jeans and a sweater. Emma stepped inside, leaning in to kiss Sarah on the cheek.

"Is this all right?" Sarah asked.

Emma stepped back and scanned Sarah from head to toe. "Fabulous!"

"Where are we going?"

"It's a surprise, but you'll love it," Emma enthused. Emma opened the passenger door to her car for Sarah and waited until she was settled before walking around to the driver's side and climbing in. "There's a wonderful little park not far from the piers. There won't be many people there and it's a great spot for my surprise."

"You're driving so I'm placing myself entirely in your hands."

"That's a dangerous thing to say," Emma flirted as she pulled away from the curb.

Twenty minutes later, Emma swung her vehicle into a deserted, snow-covered parking area. Sarah could hear the sound of Emma's snow boots rushing around the car to open the door.

Sarah laughed at how red Emma's cheeks had become. "So what's this big surprise?" Sarah asked.

Emma opened the back hatch of her SUV and pulled out a large toboggan. Her eyes glittered as she looked at the sled.

Sarah backed up and shook her finger at Emma. "Oh, no, bucko. You can't seriously believe I'm getting on that thing."

"Of course! I'll be with you. Come on before every kid in the area shows up." Emma set the toboggan on the snow and ran it back and forth. "This particular area is off limits to sleds which are much more likely to get out of control."

"I haven't been on a toboggan or a sled since I was a kid," Sarah said. "Didn't I tell you I gave up skiing?"

"This isn't skiing. The worst that could happen would be that you'd roll off. Just hang onto me," Emma said.

"Unless we run into a tree."

"Come on, Miss Negativity. I'm a doctor in case you get a nasty boo-boo. I'm a very safe toboggan driver. Please," Emma whined as she moved closer to Sarah.

Despite her skepticism, Sarah eventually carefully sat behind Emma and wrapped her arms around her waist. Emma laughed wickedly. "You only wanted me to ride this deathtrap with you so I'd have to put my arms around you," Sarah teased.

Emma glanced over her shoulder. "I only look stupid," she said, crossing her eyes. "There is a method to my madness."

Emma rocked back and forth a moment and Sarah felt the toboggan begin to slide forward. "Oh, shit!" she yelped as their weight launched it down the hill. She closed her eyes and tightened her grip around Emma as she planted her head solidly against her companion's back. She was certain she hadn't taken a single breath until she felt their momentum begin to slow.

"Want to try it again with your eyes open this time?" Emma kidded. "I won't even ask you to help me drag it back up the hill."

"That wasn't as fast as I thought it would be," Sarah said as she managed to roll off and stand up.

"It's basically the same as a bunny hill, for beginners."

"Well, that's insulting," Sarah said with a frown.

"Want to try something a little more challenging?"

Sarah cocked her head and placed her hands on her hips. "If you can do it, so can I."

"Is that a dare I hear?"

"Possibly."

"Will you keep your eyes open this time?"

Sarah gulped as she looked down the toboggan run that began farther up the hill and wished she hadn't practically dared Emma to attempt it.

"I figure we can conquer this hill before we go higher," Emma said. "It's the intermediate hill." She made herself comfortable and waited for Sarah to join her. Once Sarah's arms were wrapped around her waist Emma looked over her shoulder. "There's a bump about halfway down so we might be airborne for a half second. You okay with that?"

Sarah nodded and tightened her grip as the toboggan inched closer to the drop-off. She managed to keep her eyes open as she breathed in the cold air. This isn't so bad she thought a moment before she felt the toboggan launch off the ground and re-land on the snow. Emma guided them smoothly down the remainder of the hill and eventually extended her legs to bring them to a full stop.

"See. That wasn't bad at all," Emma said. "There's a curve on the highest hill."

Sarah climbed off and rubbed her butt. "Next time I'm bringing a cushion," she said.

"Are you getting cold?" Emma asked. "I know a place that has hot chocolate to die for. We can come back after we warm up a little."

"I'd love to warm up, but I'll pass on a repeat down the hill today. Let me get over the bruises I already have first."

Emma laughed and followed Sarah on the trek back up the hill to the car. The rest of the afternoon the two women chatted comfortably, and Sarah couldn't remember the last time she'd laughed so much. Emma drove Sarah home to change for dinner and borrowed the guest room to change her own clothes. Their conversation continued through dinner accompanied by a light white wine. After spending part of the day outdoors in the snow, the wine, along with the dim, warm interior of the restaurant made Sarah sleepy. When they left to walk back to Emma's car, Emma took Sarah's hand and tucked it over her arm. The cold air woke Sarah up and she was glad. The true sign of old age was falling asleep on your date at nine o'clock in the evening.

Emma walked Sarah to the door of the brownstone and Sarah invited her in for a cup of coffee. Emma asked questions about the history of the old house and listened to Sarah as she debated whether or not to sell it.

"The Back Bay is a very expensive area," Sarah said as they sat on the sofa. "All of these brownstones are nearly a century old."

"Hopefully you'll find a buyer with money to burn. It's really a shame that you have to part with it."

"I don't have to, but unless I decide to rent out the upper floors to college kids, there's no way I can live in the whole house. Who knows? In a few years I might not be able to make it up all those stairs unless I install an elevator," she laughed.

Emma reached over and brushed Sarah's hair off her forehead with her fingertips. "You've got lots of years before that happens, Sarah. You're still a young woman as well as a beautiful one."

"Thank you," Sarah said as she blushed. "Actually, I did start to feel young when we zipped down that hill today. I'd forgotten what it felt like."

"I'd be glad to show you other ways to feel young," Emma said, her voice husky. She cleared her throat and finished her coffee.

"What did you have in mind? Bobsledding next time?"

Emma turned to face Sarah and rested her arm along the back of the sofa. "I think that might be a little out of my league," Emma said. "Perhaps we can find something slightly more tame. In a couple of months the weather should be good enough to go sailing."

"Right," Sarah said. "Me and the Dramamine. Would you like more coffee?"

"No, thanks," Emma said. "I should head back to my place."

"Thank you for a wonderful day," Sarah said as she leaned forward to hug Emma. When Sarah released her, she saw Emma's eyes as they turned stormy. She rested her hand on Emma's arm and asked, "Are you all right?"

"Yeah, I'm fine," Emma managed. She brought her hand up and caressed Sarah's cheek before slipping the hand behind Sarah's neck. She leaned closer, searching Sarah's face for a moment before their lips met. Emma pulled away slightly, and Sarah drew her back into another, more lingering kiss. As Sarah's lips parted, Emma wrapped her in an embrace and moaned as her tongue explored the warmth of Sarah's mouth.

As the kiss ended, Emma held Sarah in a soft embrace, her hands beginning to roam over her body. It had been so long since she had been touched, and Sarah began to feel dizzy.

"You're so beautiful," Emma whispered hotly into Sarah's ear as her hand moved under Sarah's sweater. "Your body is so hot," she murmured as her fingers spread over Sarah's abdomen.

As much as Sarah wanted to be touched, she began to draw away. She stopped the movement of Emma's hands. "I...I can't," she said.

Emma took a ragged breath. "I'm sorry. I shouldn't have..."

"I thought I was ready to move on."

"I can wait. If you'd be willing to see me again."

"Of course I want to see you again. I can't promise anything more. I need a friend more than a lover right now."

Chapter Twelve

PAULINE THREW HERSELF into taking care of business at the bookstore to fill her time. Even when Kelley was away, she had never felt such a compulsion to use the store as a way to occupy her time. Jolie, as well as other friends, had done everything they could to pry her away even for an evening, but she had refused.

Now she sat in her small office, running her fingers through her hair. She had been staring at the same list of numbers for nearly an hour without actually reading them. Frustrated at her inability to suddenly not be able to concentrate, she logged onto her computer to begin compiling an order for the following week. She was sure Suzanne would have suggestions or customer orders to include.

A tap at her office door distracted her from her effort to concentrate. Pauline glanced up in time to see Jolie step inside. She stood up and went around her desk to draw her friend into a warm embrace.

"Put everything away," Jolie said. "We're going to dinner."

"I can't, sweetie. I have a hundred things to get done."

"Unless there's a book fairy who'll drop by to do your work, it will all still be on your desk tomorrow," Jolie teased. "Your friends miss you, and I've been ordered to kidnap you for tonight."

Pauline laughed. "All right, all right. But it's only to prevent you from acquiring a criminal record. Where are we going?"

"The Captain's Table."

Pauline looked down at her clothing. "Let me run upstairs to change."

"You look fine. Quit stalling and let's go."

Pauline followed Jolie out of the office and toward the front door. She paused for a moment at the counter. "Call me if anything comes up, Suzanne."

"I will. Have fun," her clerk said.

Pauline glanced at her wristwatch. "I may be back before you close."

Jolie leaned around Pauline and said, "No, she won't."

Midway through dinner, Pauline finally began to relax. As much as she didn't want to admit it, Jolie was right. She needed to be out, enjoying the company of her friends again. When the cell phone in her jacket pocket chirped, she reached for it automatically. Jolie's hand on her arm stopped her.

"No business tonight," Jolie warned.

Pauline saw the number on the phone's small screen. "I have to take this. It's my sister." She left the table as she spoke softly into the phone. She exited the restaurant and leaned against the brick wall outside. A few minutes later Pauline returned to the table.

"Is everything all right?" Jolie asked.

"My mother is in the hospital in Quebec. I told my sister I would fly home tomorrow. I'm sorry. I didn't mean to ruin this wonderful evening."

"It's nothing you can control. I'll take you to the airport. Now, let's enjoy the rest of our meal before you go home to pack. Do you know how long you'll be gone?"

"No idea. My mother has pneumonia and, at over eighty, there's no telling how long it will take her body to respond to the treatments."

PAULINE'S SISTER, CLAUDETTE, waved when she spotted her stepping off the escalator at the airport in Quebec. They hadn't seen one another in nearly three years, but had spoken on the phone every month or two. Pauline stepped into a welcoming embrace. Claudette was four years younger than Pauline, but they shared enough features that made it obvious they were related.

"I'm sorry I had to call you," Claudette said as they separated.

"You could have called me sooner. How is she?"

"Giving the doctors a terrible time. You know how she can be."

"I suppose that's a good sign. Maybe she'll want out so badly that she'll cooperate."

"How have you been since Kelley's...since you've been alone? I know I've said it before, but I liked her very much. She was good for you."

Pauline curled an arm around Claudette's shoulders and gave her a light squeeze. "Yes, she was. She liked you and Mama, too."

"I'll stop at Mama's on the way to the hospital so you can freshen up and take in your luggage."

"How are Alfred and the children?"

"Alfred is fine, and you won't recognize your niece and nephew. I think they grow taller each month. Perhaps you can have dinner with us while you're home."

Although Pauline would enjoy visiting with Claudette's children, she could only hope an evening with her brother-in-law wouldn't result in the usual disagreeable conversation. Alfred Charbonneau was a pompous ass in Pauline's generous opinion.

PAULINE DREW IN a deep breath as she stepped off the elevator behind Claudette and followed her down the corridor leading to her mother's hospital room. Halfway down the hallway, they saw a nurse leave Bernadette Reynaud's room.

"From the look on the nurse's face I'd guess Mama is having a non-cooperative day," Claudette said. "Maybe you can calm her down."

Pauline tried to look cheerful when she entered her mother's room and walked directly to the bed. "*Bonjour*, Mama," she said softly as she leaned down to kiss Bernadette's forehead. Her mother seemed unnaturally frail, her body thin beneath the bedcover. When had she begun to relinquish her once tall, slender body to time? The shining auburn hair Pauline remembered from her childhood was now gray and plaited into a long braid that rested over her shoulder. When she looked up at Pauline her vibrant eyes had a washed out, milky appearance.

"Ah, Pauline," Bernadette said. "You must convince my doctor to send me home. I cannot sleep in this contraption they call a bed."

"I will speak to him, but I cannot promise it will be today," Pauline said. "How are you feeling, Mama?"

"Like a pin cushion," Bernadette replied.

Pauline took her mother's hand in her own and brought it to her lips. Raised blue veins stood out against the thin, translucent skin on the backs of her mother's hands. Years of hard work had left her fingers slightly gnarled, yet her grip was strong.

The next morning Pauline sat in a chair beside her mother's bed, watching her sleep peacefully. Her breathing seemed shallow, but not labored. The morning nurse stepped quietly into the room and walked to the side of the bed. She gently placed her stethoscope against Bernadette's chest and listened.

"She's much better this morning," she said softly to Pauline. "It's possible she will be released in another day or two."

"I know she can be difficult."

"She's been much calmer since you arrived. It will help her recover more quickly."

"I suspect she was lonely," Pauline said. "My sister has to take care of her own family and cannot spend as much time with her as she'd like."

"There's coffee at the nurse's station, if you'd like some," the nurse offered.

"Thank you," Pauline said as she stood. "If she wakes let her know I'll be right back."

Pauline filled a Styrofoam cup with coffee and added a packet of sugar and two small containers of liquid creamer. She was grateful to see the coffee turn a lighter mocha color. As she returned to her mother's room, an older woman pushing a cart stopped near her.

"Would you care for a newspaper to read while you're waiting?" the woman asked.

Pauline looked through the stack of newspapers. Her fingers paused when she saw a copy of *The Boston Globe*. She pulled it from the stack and thanked the volunteer. She stopped next to Bernadette's bed and tenderly smoothed her hair away from her face before resuming her vigil. She sipped her coffee and began reading the front page of her newspaper. She slowly worked her way through the various sections, shifting occasionally to a more comfortable position.

"How's our patient doing today?" the doctor's voice boomed as he entered the room.

Bernadette stirred in her bed and blinked her eyes open.

"I'm taking you off the IV antibiotics today, Bernadette," he said as he gently patted her hand. "But, I'm going to leave the IV site in place in case you begin running a fever today or tonight. If you don't, I think I can send you home tomorrow with oral antibiotics. Will that work?"

Bernadette nodded and glanced at Pauline. Pauline joined them at the bed and stroked her mother's hair. "I'll have to tell Mrs. Gerard. She's anxious to get her homemade soup into you."

"It's better than penicillin," Bernadette said.

"Mama's neighbor is convinced it can cure anything," Pauline said to the doctor.

"Probably true. When she goes home, she will need to be on a light diet for a few days anyway," he said.

"That's because they try to kill you in here with what can only loosely be called food," Bernadette smirked. "I never knew there was such a thing as tasteless Jell-O."

"It's a plot," the doctor said. "If the food is bad enough, it may force our patients to recover more quickly."

Pauline pulled her chair closer to the bed after the doctor left the room.

"How are you, Pauline?" Bernadette asked.

"I am fine, Mama."

"It is difficult to be alone," Bernadette commented. "When I lost your papa, I don't know what I would have done if not for you and Claudette. But now you are alone."

"I have many friends who see that I am not lonely, Mama," Pauline said warmly.

"Yes, but they do not sleep next to you every night."

"Kelley was gone for long periods of time, so I was alone some of the time."

"You knew she would be back though. You are still a young woman. If you live as long as I have, are you prepared to live the next thirty years alone?"

"It's too soon, Mama. For now we need to concentrate on getting you better."

"Go home and get some rest."

"Claudette will be here after lunch. I will be back late this afternoon and stay until you fall asleep."

Two hours later Pauline drove her sister's vehicle back to her mother's home. She kicked her shoes off inside the front door, the same way she had been taught to do as a child and made her way into the kitchen. A cup of hot tea and a sandwich and then she would lie down until she relieved her sister. She remembered the vigil they had all kept when her father was dying and the time she had spent sitting in the ICU with Kelley. At least this time, her mother would be coming home again. Bernadette was eighty-eight years old. How many more years would it be before Pauline once again found herself waiting for the inevitable?

She set her tea and sandwich on the scarred kitchen table. She discarded the sections of the newspaper she had already read and opened the next section, spreading it out in front of her. She chewed slowly as she read the wedding announcements. She held the half sandwich in her mouth as she turned the page. She used her hand to smooth a wrinkle and stared at the picture and caption that accompanied an article about a charity event in Boston the night before. She removed the sandwich from her mouth and blinked hard as Sarah's smiling face looked up at her from the page.

Pauline knew Sarah's eyes couldn't possibly be twinkling in the photograph, that it was only the reflection of a flashbulb. She frowned when she noticed an arm wrapped possessively around Sarah's waist. Quickly, she read the caption beneath the frozen moment. *Mrs. Sarah Champion and her frequent companion, Dr. Emma Rodgers...* Frequent? Pauline looked closely at the photograph, at the woman with Sarah. A handsome woman with silver hair, looking at Sarah with... With what? Adoration? A promise of passion when they were alone?

Pauline had seen the promise of passion in Sarah's eyes, if only for a few moments. She pushed the paper away, not wanting to see that look associated with another woman. Well, what did you expect, Pauline? That Sarah would sit at home waiting for you to realize you might have made a mistake? No! It would have been a mistake. I did the right thing, Pauline argued with herself. I did the right thing.

She pulled the paper closer again and stared at it. Sarah looked beautiful. Pauline lightly ran her fingers over the photograph. She closed her eyes and remembered the softness of Sarah's skin, the scent of her blonde hair, the taste of her lips. It had been a little less than a year since that night at the cabin in the mountains. The night that could have changed Pauline's life. Why hadn't she at least called Sarah to make sure she was all right?

What would have been the purpose? She would never have been able to tell Sarah how she felt. How much she had wanted to express her feelings that night. Now so much time had passed, and Sarah had obviously moved forward. Pauline's chance had been lost.

Pauline stayed with her mother for a week before she planned to return to Vancouver. Each day seemed to be a step into the past. Bernadette had reached a time in her life when she found happiness more in the past than the present. Pauline wondered if that would be her fate as well.

Chapter Thirteen

THE NEXT FOUR months flew by in a flurry of activity for Sarah. The repairs on the brownstone had begun, and she and Emma took weekend trips once the weather began to improve. She discovered she enjoyed sailing and became Emma's first mate, raising and lowering sails and helping make occasional repairs when needed. Emma's sailboat was equipped with sleeping quarters, an adequate galley, and a bathroom. Most importantly, Sarah never suffered from bouts of sea sickness.

Although she felt comfortable being with Emma, the intimacy between them had never progressed beyond kissing and minor groping. Sarah enjoyed Emma's touches, but hadn't been swept off her feet. Sarah couldn't help but wonder whether her lingering feelings for Kelley were preventing her from allowing Emma to get closer. Emma Rodgers was everything a woman of her age could possibly want as a potential partner. She was polite, appropriately affectionate, well grounded, and reliable. Just like your average Boy Scout, Sarah thought.

In mid-June the weather was hot and typically humid. Sarah had agreed to a late afternoon golf date with Cherish. There was nothing she could do other than sit and think which always led her into depressing thoughts. On a whim she decided to surprise Emma by dropping by the hospital in hopes of whisking her away for lunch. Sarah dressed casually in a lightweight seersucker outfit that would be appropriate for her golf match with her daughter.

Sarah had been thinking more and more about her relationship with Emma. Perhaps it was time to finally move forward, she thought as she stepped off the elevator on the sixth floor of the clinic which was attached to the main hospital. As she wandered toward the appointment desk of the obstetrics and gynecology section she saw Angela walking out of an examination room accompanied by a very pregnant young woman. Angela laughed at something the woman said as they stopped at the appointment desk. Angela pulled a clipboard from a rack on the desk and flipped through the papers attached to it. She looked up, saw Sarah, and motioned for her mother-in-law to join her. They shared a warm embrace before Angela released her to say goodbye to her previous patient.

"What brings you to the wonderful world of pregnant women, Mom?" Angela asked. "I know you don't need my services."

"I thought I'd stop by and see if Emma is free for lunch," Sarah said.

Angela looked around and glanced at a board hanging behind the appointment desk. "According to the scheduling board she left for lunch about twenty minutes ago. I'm sure she'll be upset that she missed you."

"Are you free to join me? It would give us a chance to catch up."

"I have to see one more patient before I can leave. I can't be gone long though so I hope you'll be able to handle cafeteria cuisine," Angela laughed and squeezed Sarah's shoulder. "If you can wait in the reception area I'll be with you in about fifteen minutes. It's just a weekly check up."

Angela took a deep, cleansing breath as she scooted her chair closer to the table and shook out a napkin for her lap. "How have you been, Sarah? It's been a while since we've seen you."

"It's not an extremely exciting life, but I'm getting there a little at a time," Sarah said as she opened a packet of dressing and squeezed the contents over her salad.

"I assume that you're still seeing Emma."

"We've spent quite a bit of time together, but it's nothing serious. I like her very much though."

"I'm glad your life is returning to normal. How are the repairs going on the house?"

"Amazingly well. There were a couple of things I thought might be problems, but turned out to be nothing. I'm thinking about repainting the whole place to freshen it up. It's been years since the last time Kelley and I painted it."

"Are you still planning to sell it?"

"I can't make up my mind. It seems silly to move and have to pay for another place to live when the brownstone is already paid for. On the other hand, it seems silly to live in a home that large alone."

"You could close off the top two floors or possibly renovate them to create a nice apartment you could rent out."

"I could, but only if my contractor could create a second entrance."

"I'm sure they could come up with something so you could maintain your privacy."

They finished their meals in silence before Sarah walked with Angela to the elevators and they hugged one another, promising to get together again soon for a family night.

Sarah stopped in the hallway near the front entrance to rummage around in her purse for her car keys and sunglasses. She slipped her sunglasses on and started toward the exit. Before she stepped outside she saw Emma walking up the front sidewalk toward the clinic accompanied by another woman also wearing a white lab coat. Emma laughed at something the woman said and reached out to wrap her arm around the woman's waist. Not far from the entrance was a visitor seating area surrounded by well-trimmed shrubbery. Emma looked around and took the woman by the arm, pulling her into the semi-secluded area. The two women stood facing one another for a moment before Sarah saw Emma caress the woman's cheek and lean closer. Her eyes widened as the two kissed and let their hands roam freely over one another's bodies. The kiss became intense and greedy as they entwined their arms around each other. Sarah closed her eyes, no longer able to view the passion she sensed between them.

Finally, Sarah opened her eyes to see Emma and her companion parting company, their fingers touching until the last possible moment. Emma looked over her shoulder as the glass doors slid silently open and then stepped inside, a satisfied expression on her face. She stopped when she saw Sarah standing a few feet away, glaring at her.

"Sarah," Emma said. "What brings you down here?"

"I thought I might convince you to go to lunch, but I see you've already been."

"There's a new café a couple of blocks from here. I thought I'd try it out. If I'd known you were coming I would have waited for you."

"Did you eat alone?"

Emma looked at the floor and sighed before answering. "From the look on your face I'd say you already know the answer to that question."

"Who is she?"

"An old friend."

"And apparently a very close one," Sarah snapped.

"I met her before Melanie died. She helped me through some very rough days."

"And nights?"

"No! There was never anything between us until recently," Emma said roughly.

"Since you and I began seeing one another?"

"What do you want me to say Sarah? Don't accuse me of cheating on you. There has never been anything between us except friendship and, frankly, I don't think there ever will be. You can't let go of the past long enough to let anyone else into your life. It's been four frustrating months since I met you and we've had some great times, but I can't compete with a memory."

"She betrayed me," Sarah said softly. She felt tears building and willed them not to fall. "Now you have, too."

Emma reached out and placed her hand on Sarah's arm. "I'm

sorry, Sarah."

Sarah raised her chin slightly. "You'd better get back to work," she said.

Sarah left the hospital and walked stoically to her car. She opened the door and slid behind the steering wheel. She felt the tears she'd been holding back fall and roll down her cheeks as she leaned her head against the head rest. "Why can't I let you go?" she muttered. "I hate being alone like this, sweetheart."

A few minutes later she wiped the moisture from her face and left the hospital, driving toward the country club to meet Cherish. She frowned. Seeing Emma with another woman was bad enough. Now she could look forward to a few hours of Cherish's attitude. What had she done to deserve such punishment?

Sarah pulled into a parking space near the club house and dragged her golf bag from the rear compartment. It had been months since she last played golf, probably not since the last time Kelley had been home and alive. Now the weight of the bag and clubs felt heavy and unfamiliar. She was getting out of shape, but intended to stop sitting around like a fucking old woman and rejoin the world of the living. She trudged up the front steps and pulled the door open. The first thing she saw was Cherish as she stood to greet her.

"Walk or ride?" Cherish asked lightly.

"Walk," Sarah said firmly.

"I signed us up for the last tee time of the day so we don't have to worry about anyone coming up behind us."

"Did you bring the glow-in-the-dark balls in case we end up spending the night out there?"

"We've got at least four hours, Mom. Surely that will be enough time," Cherish said as she picked up her golf bag and followed Sarah out the back doors and toward the first tee. They flipped a coin to determine who went first and Sarah won. Since she had left the hospital her mind had been engaged in a war within itself. She had obviously lost Emma and any chance they might have had to establish a relationship. Could she have prevented that from happening? Well, of course she could have, she thought as she pushed her tee and ball into the ground. She stood and addressed the ball after taking a few practice swings. I could have dragged her into my bedroom and let her fuck my brains out, she screamed at herself silently as she slammed the driver into the helpless, dimpled victim of her sudden rage. Out of habit more than anything else, her eyes followed the path of the ball as it hit the fairway, bounced and rolled an additional twenty yards.

"Damn, Mom!" Cherish said. "Did you eat your Wheaties today or what? That has to be at least two hundred yards. Maybe two-fifty."

Cherish struck her drive solidly and in perfect form, but still ended up behind Sarah's ball. During the first nine holes, Sarah railed at herself for all the stupid mistakes she had made over the years. Drive. She had unwittingly alienated Cherish because of her relationship with Kelley, thinking mostly of her own happiness. Drive. She had trusted Kelley, never dreaming she shared her life with another woman. Drive. She had very nearly made a fool of herself with Pauline because of her loneliness. Drive. She had met and lost Emma because of her refusal to trust again and open herself up to another woman. The truth was she didn't know how to open up. Kelley was the only woman she had ever been with intimately. Drive. She was too damn old to start over again.

The only times Sarah's angry thoughts changed were when she was putting. Each time she took a deep breath and brought up a pleasant memory in an attempt to override her anger. She remembered all the times she felt adored and wanted by Kelley. Perhaps it was a good thing that she wouldn't be seeing Emma again. Emma made her feel wanted, but never adored. Thoughts of all the Christmases she, Kelley, and the children had spent in Vermont. The snowmen they built and dressed. The mistletoe Kelley insisted on hanging anywhere she thought Sarah might stand. Occasionally, Sarah missed a put because of the moistness that blurred her vision.

Because there was no other group following them, Cherish and Sarah decided to take a breather after the ninth hole.

"Well, you're certainly kicking my ass," Cherish said as she added up their score cards. "If you keep this up on the back nine you'll be way under par for the course. Have you ever done that before?"

"No," Sarah said. "Just having a good day, I guess. I'll probably fall apart in the second half."

Cherish reached over and placed her hand on Sarah's knee. "Are you all right, Mom?"

"I'm fine. Am I acting strange?"

"A little. We've been together about an hour and a half and haven't argued once. Don't you find that strange?"

"We shouldn't argue all the time. Now that Kelley's gone, we don't have anything to argue about," Sarah said with a shrug.

"I thought you were seeing someone new. Another woman."

"Not anymore."

"When did that happen?"

"Today."

"No good in the sack?"

Sarah turned and stared at her daughter. "We never, as you've so indelicately put it, hit the sack," Sarah said indignantly.

"Well, there's your problem then," Cherish exclaimed. "You need to get laid."

"You mean by a man, I suppose," Sarah grunted.

"Whoever. Man or woman. If a woman does it for you and puts a spring in your step again, I can learn to live with that."

"Too bad you couldn't think that way years ago. We'd both have been much happier."

"It's the same as any other relationship, isn't it? So this new woman didn't rotate your rudder. There are others out there who might."

Sarah turned her body to face her daughter. "I appreciate your concern for my sexual well-being, dear, but I'm not looking for someone to replace Kelley. She was the first and only woman I've ever been with. What we did in the privacy of our room, while wonderful and certainly fulfilling, was only a part of our relationship. I loved her as a person, and I wish you could have known her as I did. She was a very gentle woman with a tender nature. She treated me like a queen and I loved her for that."

"Yet she ended up hurting you."

"Yes. Yes, she did. She hurt me very badly. I don't know if I'll ever trust anyone completely again. There are some secrets that should never be known."

Cherish squinted and looked at the still blue sky above them. "I have a secret. Sometimes secrets should be known before it's too late, and you can't tell anyone."

"You can tell me anything."

"If I tell you, will you promise not to tell anyone else? I wouldn't want to damage my reputation."

"I promise."

"I admired Kelley very much. She was a woman working in a man's world and she was successful at it. She was a role model for other women and, no matter what our disagreements were, I respected her for that."

"When did you come to that conclusion?"

"When I grew up, probably ten or twelve years ago," Cherish said with a shrug. "I don't know exactly. One of those rare days when I engaged in more than shallow thinking."

"I wish Kelley had known that."

"I wish I'd told her. It's something I'll always regret. I think I was jealous because I couldn't make you as happy as she did."

"You made me happy in a different way. I haven't always been happy with you, Cherish, but I've always loved you. I always will. You're a part of me, just as Carl is. Kelley knew that."

"She was a part of you too."

"Not in the same way. I think she knew that if I was forced to choose between you and Carl and her, she might lose."

"Oh, come on, Mother! You'd never have left Kelley."

"I nearly did once," Sarah said, glancing absently through the trees. "Actually, I think she almost left me."

"I didn't know that."

"Of course you didn't. You were a child and we were the adults. It was up to us to make the best decision we could."

"What happened?"

Sarah took a deep breath. "We were arguing, something we rarely did. I don't remember exactly what you did, but Kelley was livid. She wasn't angry with me, but was very upset with whatever it was you had done. She suggested that I take you and Carl and move out. Find a place as close to the brownstone as possible for the three of us. Then when you two were at school either I could go to the brownstone, or she would come to where we were living. She wanted to be with me, but thought we'd both be better off if we weren't all living under the same roof. I told her she was overreacting. She needed to act like an adult, like a parent. It sort of went downhill from there."

"Why didn't you leave?"

"I'd already uprooted you and Carl twice and I didn't want to do it again."

"I threw a knife at her," Cherish admitted in a flat voice.

"What?"

"I threw a knife at her. I told myself it wasn't deliberate, but it was."

"Oh, my God, Cherish. What did she do?"

"She grabbed me by the throat and slammed me against a wall. I saw the look in her eyes and it scared me. I think it did her too. She let me go and locked herself in her study."

"Why didn't you tell me?"

"Like any kid, I didn't want to get in trouble. I kept waiting for the other shoe to drop after you came home, but nothing ever happened. I thought she'd tell you."

"She didn't want to get in trouble either, I guess. I knew things were bad, but not that bad. That's probably the same night she suggested we not live together."

"I'm sorry I made your lives so miserable, Mom. I was a stupid kid."

"Yeah, you were. I sure wish we could have had this discussion while Kelley was around to hear it." Sarah stood and stretched. "Ready to tackle the rest of the course?"

"I'll have to hope it's kinder than the first half."

"Just take out your frustrations on the ball. That's what I've been doing," Sarah admitted. "Now that we've had this talk I'll probably play like shit."

Cherish laughed. "I love it when you curse, Mother. It's so out of character."

Sarah winked at her daughter. "Then you don't know me as well as you think you do."

OVER THE NEXT several months Sarah began making contact again with old friends and attending meetings for organizations she belonged to. She spent more time with Cherish and her family. Although she no longer owned the cabin in Vermont, she rented a small lodge outside of Stowe the next winter and surprised Cherish and Carl and their families with a long weekend ski trip. Ethan was past due learning to ski, and she didn't mind slowly making her way with her grandson down the beginner slopes while the other adults attempted the more challenging hills nearby.

She regretted letting the cabin go, but, truthfully, it was unlikely any of them would make enough trips to the area to justify keeping it. In the evenings, Carl started a fire in the fire pit on the outside deck, and they all sat close to the warmth, drinking coffee and chatting. Much to Sarah's dismay, the old cabin could be seen through the main window of the lodge, nestled in the trees on the mountain. At night she could see lights inside glimmering through the bare trees and down the snow. She missed the cabin and wished she was there, looking down over the ski resort with warm arms wrapped around her. She hoped it was as special to its new owner as it had been to her.

The economy and the real estate market in Boston had taken a downturn Sarah's realtor hadn't anticipated, and Sarah decided not to sell the brownstone. The time wasn't right. Only the first and second floors were being lived in, but Sarah had purchased some new furniture and had the walls repainted in warm and inviting colors. She slowly began inviting friends over for dinner and even hosted a Christmas party for the staff who worked with Angela at the hospital, including Emma and her new girlfriend, Elizabeth.

To welcome in the New Year, Sarah, assisted by Cherish and Angela, threw a party for their family and close friends. For the first time since Kelley's death, laughter once again filled the old house. Suddenly overcome with emotion, Sarah retreated into the kitchen. When Cherish came into the room, she found Sarah leaning over the counter with tears streaming down her face.

"What's wrong, Mom?" Cherish asked anxiously, setting her glass on the counter.

"Nothing. Everything's perfect."

"Then why are you crying?"

"Because I'm happy. Can't you feel it, Cherish?"

"Feel what? How much punch have you had tonight?"

"Kelley's watching us and she's happy everything's back to the way it should be."

Cherish looked up at the ceiling and picked her glass up and raised it. "You can go away now, Kelley," she said. Looking back at her mother she added, "We miss you, but we're all fine."

"I do miss you, baby" Sarah said. She wrapped her arms around Cherish and pulled her into a tight hug.

Chapter Fourteen

SARAH BEGAN TO fill her time once again with charity work and various women's groups that had once occupied her while Kelley was away from home. The group she enjoyed most was her women's reading group. Once an avid reader, she hadn't read as much since Kelley's death. Once a month, she welcomed the dozen or more women into her home and took part in spirited discussions about the merits of their book of the month. She didn't like every selection, but enjoyed most of them. The unofficial leader of their group was a woman about Sarah's age named Margaret Cohen, the owner of the women's bookstore in Northampton. Originally the group had met in the bookstore, but as it grew in number it became too crowded. Margaret had been grateful when Sarah volunteered her home as a meeting place.

Sarah set out snacks and drinks for the women and looked around to make sure there were enough places for everyone to sit. When the chimes in the hallway rang she rushed to the front door. As usual Margaret stood outside holding a large box in her arms. Each month Margaret brought in stacks of new books for the group to consider as future reading selections.

"Looks like a bumper crop," Sarah said as Margaret wrangled to box into the living room.

"It is," Margaret said, dropping the box onto the carpet with a thud. "It seems like every publisher, large or small, is putting out more books. Of course that's good for us, but they weigh a damn ton."

"I have a table we can move in here to display them all if you'll help me carry it."

"No problem," Margaret said. She followed Sarah into the study, grabbing a small sandwich on the way and stuffing it into her mouth.

"Hungry?" Sarah asked.

"Starving! I didn't have time to stop for dinner before I came over."

"I can fix you something before the others arrive. I have leftover pot roast in the refrigerator."

"That sounds scrumptious."

"First the table, and I'll heat it up while you get the books set out."

Fifteen minutes later Margaret leaned back in the kitchen chair and wiped her mouth with her napkin.

"That was delicious, Sarah," she said. "Maybe we should start a women's cooking group. Now I won't have to worry about my stomach grumbling through the book discussion tonight. You're a life saver."

"At least I won't have to throw it out. After cooking for four all those years, it's hard to just cook for one."

"I wouldn't know. I've cooked for one for so long a guest would have to fight me for the food. Did you like this month's book?"

"It was an interesting story. The characters were a little young for me to identify with."

"You were young once."

"Forty years ago," Sarah laughed. "I vaguely remember being twenty."

"We have three or four choices for next month that have older characters."

"You mean they're thirty?"

"Older than that. I've already read a couple and they have excellent characters and rather intriguing story lines. I had an interesting idea on the way over here tonight. Since there are so many new books out right now, I thought it might be interesting if each of us read a different one and then gave sort of a book report next meeting to let everyone know what the book was about."

"That's an interesting idea, and we would know which books we might want to read later on."

"I'll bring it up at the meeting."

After the discussion about that month's selection ended, Margaret introduced her idea to the members of the reading group, and they agreed to try it for the next month. Once everyone settled down to enjoy the refreshments and chat before making their selections, Sarah looked through the books that were neatly arranged on the table. Always drawn by the cover art, she picked up several books and read the blurbs on the back. One in particular caught her attention and she picked it up and flipped it over.

"I was hoping you'd choose that one," Margaret said as she joined Sarah at the table. "She used to be one of my favorites."

"Used to be?"

"She wrote three or four books and then stopped writing. No one knows why. This is her first book in nearly twenty years. I was so excited to see her name on the cover that I couldn't wait to read it."

Sarah gazed down at the lavender cover and read the author's name for the fourth or fifth time since she first picked it up. *The Far Side of Happiness* by Pauline Reynaud.

"I'll read this one," Sarah said quietly.

"You'll like it," Margaret enthused. "She's a brilliant writer, but the storyline is a little sad. It's about..."

"Coping with the loss of a loved one," Sarah finished. She blinked hard. "I...uh...read the back cover."

"Not exactly a tear jerker, but close. Are you sure you want to read it? I know you lost your wife a couple of years ago."

"No, it's fine," Sarah said with a cheerfulness she didn't really feel.

THAT EVENING SARAH climbed the stairs to her second floor bedroom, carrying the book with her. She placed it on her nightstand and went through her usual evening ritual before turning the bedcovers down and settling down for the night. Placing her reading glasses on her nose, she ran a hand over the book cover for a moment. She was almost afraid to open the book. Although her greatest moments of sadness had passed, an occasional memory was brought to the surface by an unexpected event. The dedication brought a lump to Sarah's throat. *To K.C. and the life we shared.*

Sarah read until her eyes refused to remain open another minute. It was hours past her normal bed time. She placed the book on the nightstand and lay in the dark going through what she'd already read. She wondered how much of the story was fictional and how much sprang from Pauline's personal memories. There was no mistaking the main characters as anyone other than Kelley and Pauline, and as she read, Kelley's face appeared in her mind.

It took Sarah three nights to finish reading the book. As she turned the last page she wished it would go on, but the story had reached its logical conclusion. The message in the story was clear. Grieving never ends. It stays with us, buried beneath new memories and occasionally makes an appearance when we least expect it. Time gradually smoothes the edges of pain, leaving one with the ability to continue living with only blunted pain.

Sarah placed the book on her abdomen and removed her reading glasses. She felt the niggling itch of tears as her mind went through the scenes of the book. Be impartial, she thought. It was a touching story, sad, but with the hope that the main character would recoup and continue to build her life, adding more layers. There had been only one scene that had disturbed Sarah. It recalled the time a secondary character had spent at a cabin with the character who represented Pauline. She was touched by the tenderness of the scene. She could hear Pauline's soft accent, smell the scent of her arousal, and taste her desire as their lips met. It was erotically romantic, and Sarah wondered what would have happened if Pauline had not withdrawn. Sarah would recommend the book to the other women in her group, never telling them how true most of the story had been.

AT THE MAY meeting of Sarah's reading group Margaret announced the annual author event which would be hosted by her store, *Afterwords*, in June. Four authors had agreed to appear and give readings from their newest novels as well as spend time answering questions. Margaret was particularly excited that the author's appearances would coincide with the Pride event in Northampton. Sarah and two other ladies in the group agreed to furnish refreshments between two and five that afternoon and see that drinks were available beginning at noon.

Sarah rose early the day of the author event and took a long, leisurely shower. After a late breakfast she dressed and drove to Northampton, hoping to get a parking place within easy walking distance of the bookstore. She arrived a little before eleven and spent some time strolling up and down the streets, stopping occasionally to chat with vendors setting up tables in front of their stores.

She arrived at *Afterwords* to find Margaret and her partner running around the store, apparently without much purpose.

"Oh, Sarah!" Margaret said. "I'm so glad you arrived early. There's been a change in plans and we now have five authors."

"That's wonderful," Sarah said. "Do we need to re-arrange the seating?"

"Yes, but we had to order more refreshments. There wasn't time to call you and then for you and the others to prepare more. Lambert's just called and said our order was ready. Could you pick them up while we re-arrange?"

"Of course," Sarah said. On the way out of the bookstore she ran into another reading group member, Alice Foster, bringing refreshments and enlisted her to help carry trays from Lambert's Delicatessen, a few blocks away.

By the time Sarah and Alice returned, there were only ten minutes left before the event was scheduled to begin. Sarah was surprised to see the number of women who had already arrived at the bookstore. She and Alice replenished the sandwich trays as everyone got settled. Sarah looked around until she found a seat off to the left side of the room, not far from the tables holding food in case she needed to add more to them. At the front of the room were two long tables and five chairs.

Applause greeted Margaret, her hair pulled back in a loose

bun, as she stepped in front of the tables and began the event.

"Welcome, ladies. Today is an exciting day for us at *Afterwords*. This is the fourth year we've held what we call our author event. This year we have four new lesbian authors whom I'm sure many of you have read, and we're thrilled to welcome our fifth author back after several years away from lesbian publishing. It's my honor to introduce Melinda Crafton, Selena Marquez, Hunter McCaffrey, Celeste Young, and Pauline Reynaud."

A healthy round of applause greeted the five women as they walked toward the tables. Sarah glanced up and did a double take when she saw Pauline, dressed in a comfortable looking, lightweight, yellow summer suit accented by white earrings and a white necklace. Her auburn hair was cut shorter than Sarah remembered, at a comfortable summer length. She and the other authors waved to the women gathered to hear and meet them. Then they all sat down and looked toward the woman who had entered first. She stood and moved to the microphone set up in front of the tables and flipped open a book to a pre-marked page and began reading. Through the readings given by the first three authors, Sarah hadn't heard a word. She spent nearly forty-five minutes staring at Pauline, who was paying rapt attention to the other authors, applauding politely after each one. Pauline looked at ease and was stunning. She appeared to be much happier than the last day Sarah had seen her, nearly two years earlier.

When Pauline stood to read, she smiled and scanned the audience before beginning. Sarah prayed Pauline would not see her and leaned over to get something from her purse to avoid meeting Pauline's eyes. By the time she sat up again, Pauline had begun speaking, her softly accented voice flowing over the women in the room.

Sarah closed her eyes and could easily envision the passage Pauline was reading. She felt the desire and need as the characters kissed for the first time. She had experienced the same emotions described in the pages of *The Far Side of Happiness*. She remembered the unbearable ache she had felt inside when Kelley had left her. Many of the scenes with the partner Sarah knew to be Kelley, mirrored her own life closely. Pauline had felt the same way Sarah did about the wonderful woman who shared her life…shared both their lives. Sarah saw that the women around her were captivated by Pauline's words. But they would never know that Pauline and Sarah had shared the same woman and suffered the same grief. Only the two of them could understand one another's feelings.

Near the end of the reading, which was beautiful and moving, Pauline turned to her right and looked over the half-lens reading glasses that rested low on her nose. She stumbled slightly over the words when her eyes met Sarah's, but quickly recovered her place and continued reading. To Sarah it seemed that Pauline was reading only to her and everything around her faded away except how beautiful Pauline was. The shorter auburn hair moved, carefree and shiny, when she moved her head. Sarah felt almost abandoned as Pauline slowly turned her attention to the other side of the room. Her face in profile still looked as strong as Sarah remembered. There had been times over the past months when something happened that reminded Sarah of the weekend they'd spent together at the cabin. The way Pauline looked at her had taken her breath away. Pauline had desired her. Sarah was sure of it, even though Pauline had chosen to deny her feelings. Sarah wondered what would have happened, how her life would have changed, if she had made love with Pauline that night so many months ago. She squeezed her eyes tightly shut. She shouldn't be thinking these thoughts.

After the final author completed her reading, the audience was invited to join in a question and answer session. The questions were interesting and the responses light-hearted and occasionally humorous. Periodically, Sarah's eyes met Pauline's and Sarah had to look away. The room was becoming unbearably stuffy. Soon the women began lining up to have copies of their books signed by each author. Sarah saw her chance to escape from the store unnoticed. She could later blame it on a headache, which wouldn't have been a lie. She reached down for her purse and was startled by a hand on her shoulder.

"Because Pauline agreed to be here on such short notice, she brought copies of her book with her," Margaret said. "There's a box in the store room. Would you mind bringing it out?" Without actually waiting for an answer, Margaret patted Sarah's shoulder and disappeared. As if all the stars and planets were aligning against her, Sarah would have to face Pauline and act as if they were strangers. She had never told anyone about the unusual relationship she shared with Pauline Reynaud and never intended to. She prayed that Pauline wouldn't mention it either.

When Sarah set the books on the table, Pauline raised her head and leaned toward her. "It's wonderful to see you again, Sarah."

"I didn't know you were a writer," Sarah replied.

"There is much you do not know about me." Pauline said as Sarah removed the books from the box and stacked them on the table.

"I'm glad you could make it to our little event."

"I was in Quebec visiting my mother. She hasn't been feeling well, but I suppose that happens when you're over eighty years old."

"I hope she's all right."

"It was just a touch of bronchitis," Pauline said dismissively as she turned her attention to a woman who approached the table.

As she walked away Sarah could feel Pauline's eyes on her back. She left the bookstore quickly and leaned against the outside wall of the building before taking a deep breath. Pauline was the last person she had expected to ever see again. She rubbed her forehead and closed her eyes. She jumped when a hand touched her shoulder.

"Are you okay?" Margaret asked. "You look a little pale."

"It was getting a little stuffy and I needed some fresh air," Sarah said. "I'm sorry, but would you be very upset if I had to leave? My grandson has a baseball game this afternoon." Sarah wasn't sure whether Ethan played baseball or not, but one lie was as good as another at the moment.

"Not at all. We have it under control and the worst part is over."

SARAH DROPPED HER keys into a wooden bowl inside the front door of the brownstone and started up the stairs to her bedroom. She shook her head as her foot brought a familiar creaking sound from the fifth step. For as long as she could remember that one step had creaked. No matter what she and Kelley had tried, they hadn't been able to correct it. They finally chalked it up to the character of the house.

She set her canvas bag down and sat on the edge of her bed. She was tired, but had done nothing to cause it. It had been a leisurely day until she had gone to the bookstore. The emotions brought back by seeing Pauline again rested on her like a dead weight. She stood and began undressing hoping a nice warm shower would wash the unwanted weight away. When she pulled her polo shirt over her head, she saw the red light flashing on the answering machine next to her bed. She pushed the play button and listened to the messages while she removed her slacks and socks. Her realtor wanted to know if Sarah was still interested in selling the brownstone. She had a client who might be interested. Sarah ignored the remainder of the realtor's message and started toward the bathroom. The soft voice of the second caller stopped her in her tracks.

"Sarah, this is Pauline," the soft voice said. "I hope you do not mind, but I got this number from Margaret." There was a short pause as if Pauline was waiting for Sarah to pick up the receiver. "Sarah, I would like very much to see you. I am flying home the day after tomorrow. I am staying at the Hilton in downtown

Boston. My room number is 1209. Please call me."

Sarah stared at the answering machine and fought the urge to return Pauline's phone call. Instead she walked into the bathroom and adjusted the water temperature in the shower. It would be a mistake to see Pauline again, she told herself. The realization that she had feelings for Kelley's other widow brought tears to her eyes. Pauline had been right. Perhaps her attraction was only because of the love they had shared for the same woman. Their meeting that day had been nothing more than a fluke, a terrible accident.

Chapter Fifteen

ALMOST TWO YEARS exactly had passed as Sarah looked out over the railing of the ferry from Horseshoe Bay, north of Vancouver, to the departure bay on Vancouver Island. She couldn't remember the last time she had traveled alone. Kelley had always been with her, lending new insight to even familiar sights. Sarah felt as if she was seeing everything for the first time. The morning had begun with cool temperatures, but by midday it had become quite comfortable. The sunlight sparkled off the water and the salty smell invigorated her senses. It was mid-September and she had been in Vancouver two days, but this was the first day she had ventured out of her hotel room. It had taken her longer to find the turn-off she was looking for in Nanaimo than she thought it would, and she wished she had paid more attention when she'd accompanied Pauline to spread Kelley's ashes.

She parked her car near the abandoned church and followed the path into the woods, hoping it hadn't been altered. She was relieved when she came to the wooden footbridge across the ravine. It wasn't much farther from that point. The sun hovered over the ocean before her, and she sat on a large boulder just above the rocky outcropping she remembered from her last visit. She stretched her legs out in front of her and leaned back on her arms, basking in the last rays of sunlight descending into the blue water. She scanned the horizon in front of her and threw her head back, laughing when she saw the whales break the water. She had often wondered if their appearance each day near sunset was a daily ritual. It didn't really matter, but she was glad to see them on this trip. She doubted she would return again. She needed to say goodbye one final time. She could finally sleep without the plague of dreams that had visited her almost every night for nearly eighteen months. Over the last year, the dreams came more infrequently and were less disturbing, moving into the realm of pleasant memories.

She had come to realize that her attraction to Emma had only been driven by wanting to hurt Kelley in some way. But Kelley was gone, incapable of hurt any longer. In the end, Sarah believed she would have only hurt herself by giving up a small piece of her dignity. Emma deserved more. They both deserved so much more. Sarah had long since made her peace with Emma. She even reluctantly had to admit that she liked Emma's new girlfriend.

They had been friends while Melanie was still alive, and their renewed friendship gradually evolved into something much closer.

The last of the golden orb dropped from the sky, leaving only rays of pink and purple to penetrate the blue-gray above. Sarah stood, wiped sand from the seat of her jeans, and watched the sky slowly turn into a brilliant magenta. "This is goodbye, baby," she said. "I know you're at peace, and I have to find my new life without you to guide me. You always told me I could do anything if I set my mind to it. I think I finally believe you. It's all up to me, isn't it? I have to make my own happiness. No matter what, I'll always carry you in a special place inside me. I forgive you, and I forgive myself."

Sarah closed her eyes and raised her head, taking a deep, cleansing breath. The scent of the ocean filled her lungs and a gentle breeze carrying a soft mist climbed over the edge of the rocks around her and ruffled her hair for a moment. "I love you, too, sweetheart. Take care," she said as the moisture caressed her face.

SARAH SPENT MOST of the next morning walking around the city. The longer she walked, the more she regained a sense of peace. She sat on a bench for a few minutes, watching the people making their way up and down the street in the old section of the city. She wondered if they knew what life had in store for them. What an adventure it could be. She had forgotten that for a while.

She took a deep breath and stood up. Resolutely, she walked to the door of a little bookstore and pushed it open. The young woman behind the front counter glanced at her as she stepped inside and began making her way down the aisles. She would need something to read during the long flight home and browsed for nearly half an hour before selecting an interesting looking book. She carried it to the counter and waited for the clerk to ring up her purchase.

"This is a good book," the clerk said casually.

"I've read others by the same author and enjoyed them very much," Sarah said. When she took the package from the clerk, she asked, "Is Pauline Reynaud here today, by any chance?"

"You just missed her. She went to lunch with a friend. There's an excellent café two blocks down the street. They have sidewalk seating, and this time of year is ideal for eating outdoors," the young woman said. "That's where she usually goes."

Sarah walked casually in the direction the clerk had pointed out to her. Her breath stopped when she saw Pauline seated at an outdoor table with an attractive woman who looked like she might be in her late forties. The two women were laughing, and Sarah watched the attractive woman reach across the small round table and take Pauline's hand, slowly running her thumb across the back of it. Pauline looked down at their joined hands and crooked her lips. She leaned forward and their lips met briefly. When Pauline leaned back in her chair again her eyes came up and widened when she saw Sarah standing on the sidewalk across the street.

Sarah felt like a fool as she turned and walked quickly away. She looked over her shoulder in time to see Pauline standing on the opposite curb, waiting for cars to pass in order to cross. When she saw a taxi approaching, Sarah stepped off the curb and flagged it down, getting in as soon as she could before Pauline could catch up to her. She gave the driver the name of her hotel as he pulled away. She rummaged around in her purse for something to staunch the tears that had begun flowing down her cheeks. What had she been thinking? She hadn't heard from Pauline since the phone call three months before. The phone call Sarah hadn't returned. Did she think Pauline would be sitting at home, pining away while waiting for Sarah to show up? Obviously, since she hadn't returned the phone call in Boston, Pauline had decided to move on with her life. Just as obviously, another woman already filled her life. For an instant Sarah was furious. Pauline was betraying Kelley's memory and the knowledge of that betrayal swelled inside her.

As soon as she returned to her hotel, a small establishment located in an older, but well-kept, section of Vancouver, Sarah called and re-scheduled her ticket to leave the next morning. There were no earlier flights available or she would have left that evening, that hour.

A solid knock at Sarah's hotel room door pulled her away from her packing. She wasn't expecting anyone or anything and ignored the first knock. She didn't want to be dragged away from her foray into self-pity. But the knocking persisted and she finally walked to the door and looked through the peep-hole. She watched as a hand brushed disheveled dark auburn hair over the head of the woman pacing back and forth in front of the door.

"Go away," she said, barely loud enough to be heard. She cleared her throat and repeated the order more loudly.

"Sarah! Sarah, please open the door," Pauline's voice begged.

"No! Go away! I don't want to see you."

Finally pounding began against the door. "I'm going to stand in this hallway, disturbing the people around you until you open this damn door!" Pauline said loudly.

"I'll call downstairs and have hotel security remove you!" Sarah called back. "Leave me alone!"

"Do you know how many hotels I had to call before I found

you?" Pauline asked. "Please open the door before I humiliate both of us."

Sarah walked back to the door and cracked it open, leaving the security chain attached. Pauline stepped closer to the crack, barely able to see even half of Sarah's face. "Please, Sarah."

"What do you want? And how did you know what room I was in?" Sarah asked coldly.

"I bribed the desk clerk," Pauline said with a shrug. "I want to know why you ran away this afternoon."

"I didn't run away."

"Why didn't you return my phone call in Boston?"

"It would have been a mistake."

"You don't know that. Open the door. Please."

Sarah closed the door and rested her head against the frame, waiting several moments before she reached up and slid the chain from its latch. She turned the door knob and backed away to place distance between herself and Pauline. The door to the room opened slowly before Pauline stepped inside.

"Why did you come back to Vancouver?" Pauline asked.

"I...I made a trip back to the cliffs."

Pauline's eyes took in the partially packed suitcase lying on the bed. "Are you leaving?"

"Tomorrow morning," Sarah answered.

"Then you have already been to the cliffs."

"Yes. I came back to say goodbye."

"Have you been well?"

"Yes. I'm fine."

"I wish you would have joined me for lunch today," Pauline said.

"I didn't want to interrupt your date."

"My date? Jolie has been my best friend since I moved to Vancouver, but we have never dated. I mean, we have, but never seriously"

"Your social life is none of my business," Sarah said in a vain attempt to look indignant.

"That's right, Sarah. It isn't. Just as yours is none of my business."

"I did meet someone, but it didn't work out." Sarah stared at the floor. "Have you found someone to replace Kelley?"

"I could never replace her. I can only live my life."

"What about the woman I saw you with? Jolie. You kissed her. I saw you."

"Why would I deny that? Jolie has helped me through the worst days of my life. She is a beautiful woman, and I am grateful to have someone I can talk to."

"Does she help you at night, too?" Sarah retorted. "When you're lonely and can't sleep without someone beside you?"

"And if she did, would you be jealous?"

"Of course not! Yes!" Sarah spun away from Pauline. "It's none of my business."

"Are you still seeing that woman in Boston? Should I be jealous of your feelings for her?" Pauline asked sharply.

"What woman in Boston?" Sarah turned and demanded.

"The handsome one with the silver hair and her hands touching you. Even in a grainy newspaper photograph I could see how she looked at you. I'm not a fool, Sarah."

"Emma? I haven't seen her in over a year," Sarah said. "I couldn't give her what she wanted or needed."

"If seeing me with Jolie meant nothing to you, you wouldn't have run away like an impetuous child."

"I'm not a child." Sarah felt her eyes begin to itch as tears tried to form. She turned to pluck a tissue from the nightstand.

Pauline stepped closer and hesitated for a moment before bringing her hands up and resting them lightly on Sarah's shoulders.

"Don't," Sarah said.

"The last time we were together you wanted me to touch you," Pauline said gently.

"I was drunk!"

Pauline's hands squeezed Sarah's shoulders tighter and she brought her mouth closer to Sarah's ear. "It took every ounce of strength I had to stop touching you. Your body was..."

"Please stop," Sarah insisted. "That was a mistake. This is a mistake." She forced herself to face Pauline. "I'd like you to leave now. I have to finish packing. It was nice to see you again." With difficulty, Sarah forced her eyes up to Pauline's face. "I...I'm sorry."

"I'm so damned tired of being sorry," Pauline said as her eyes hardened. "I don't want to be sorry for what I feel anymore." She reached out and grabbed Sarah's arm, pulling her closer. Before Sarah could object, Pauline's mouth covered hers insistently. Sarah's hand came up between them and pushed against Pauline. The two women stood in a battle of wills until Pauline jerked her mouth away from Sarah's, breathing heavily.

"Sarah..." Pauline began.

The sting as Sarah's hand flew out and slapped her startled Pauline for a moment. Sarah covered her mouth when she saw the hurt in Pauline's blue eyes. Almost as quickly as it had happened, Sarah regretted her overreaction. She stepped closer in an attempt to console Pauline, but found herself pushed away. She watched as

Pauline got her emotions under control and stood up straighter.

"You are right, Sarah. It was a mistake for me to come here," Pauline said. "I was a fool to think there could be more between us than the memory of Kelley Champion. Perhaps my interest in you only stems from my desire to be close to her again. I loved her with everything I was, but she is no longer here, and she'll never be back."

"I can't stand the pain I feel inside anymore," Sarah said. "I'm afraid, Pauline. I haven't been able to stop thinking about you. But what if what I feel is only my need to be close to Kelley again? That's not fair to you, and it's not fair to me."

Pauline's eyes searched Sarah's face. Then she moved carefully toward her again, stopping in front of her and taking her face in her hands. "If either of us calls out her name when we make love, then we will know it's a mistake." Pauline brought her lips closer to Sarah's and kissed her softly. Sarah parted her lips slightly and invited Pauline into the warmth of her mouth.

As Pauline's tongue slipped inside, the heat of Sarah's mouth engulfed her and ignited her desire. When Sarah's head fell back, Pauline slid her hands beneath Sarah's pullover to touch her warm skin as she lowered her mouth to trail kisses along her throat. She drew Sarah closer, caressing her body. "If we make love now, I won't be strong enough to stop this time, Sarah," she rasped.

"When we do, I won't ask you to," Sarah said. "I...I want to be with you, Pauline, but you were right. There's so much I don't know about you."

Pauline pressed her forehead against Sarah's. "Please postpone your flight back to Boston. Give us a chance to become acquainted."

SARAH SPENT THE remainder of the afternoon with Pauline, watching her interact with customers. Pauline seemed relaxed and stopped occasionally to speak with her.

"The store will close at six o'clock," Pauline said. "There is a quiet little restaurant a few blocks from here. I thought perhaps we could talk over dinner."

"That would be nice. Or we could prepare something here."

"You would be taking your life in your hands if I cooked," Pauline said with a shrug.

"I trust you," Sarah said. "We could cook dinner together. I've always found that is a wonderful time to talk."

"I don't have much in my refrigerator, but we can go to the market."

"Are you writing anything new?"

"I have begun a manuscript, but have reached a point where I need to think about where the story is going."

"I'd love to read it," Sarah said.

"I'm sure sitting here is boring for you."

"No. I'm enjoying watching you work. You have a way of making people feel comfortable."

"Pauline," Suzanne called out.

"Excuse me. Duty calls," Pauline said as she turned toward the front counter.

Sarah leaned back in the soft upholstered chair and took a sip of the tea Pauline had given her earlier. She felt something rub against her legs and looked down to see a small, fluffy, peach-colored kitten making its way in and out of her legs. She leaned down to pick the kitten up. It made lazy circles in her lap as she stroked its soft features. It purred loudly and pressed against her hand before turning to face her. It pushed its face against her and she laughed.

"Marcel," Pauline said when she saw the pushy little kitten. "What are you doing?"

"It's all right," Sarah said. "I like cats, but Kelley was allergic to them. They're very calming."

"I found him in the alleyway behind the store a few months ago. He was very small and quite hungry. I should have known that after I fed him one time, I would never be rid of him."

"His name is Marcel?"

Pauline nodded as she leaned over and ran her hand through the kitten's fur. "He is the most relaxed cat I have ever seen. Even the veterinarian was amazed at how calm he is, especially for an abandoned cat."

"He's beautiful."

"I suppose I'm stuck with him now. He won't go away."

"He's adopted you," Sarah said.

"Hmm. I think he simply knows a sucker when he sees one," Pauline said, twisting her mouth slightly. She handed Sarah a small stack of papers. "I thought you might like to read what I've written so far. If you don't want to, that's fine."

"No. Marcel and I would be thrilled to read it," Sarah said as she took the papers.

For the next hour, Pauline periodically stopped what she was doing to glance at Sarah. The first part of the manuscript lay on the table next to her. As she read, she stroked Marcel, who was sound asleep in her lap. By the time Pauline and Suzanne closed the store for the day, Sarah had joined Marcel in a cat nap.

A light touch on her shoulder awakened Sarah. Her hands went reflexively to Marcel as she sat up. "I'm sorry," she said. "Marcel's purring lulled me off to sleep."

Pauline lifted the kitten from Sarah's lap and held him. "Let me feed him and then we can go to the market," she said.

PAULINE LEANED AGAINST the kitchen counter, chopping cucumber and green onions, while Sarah washed and sliced potatoes into a pot. Pauline noticed how at home Sarah seemed. Sarah turned the eye of the stove on and adjusted the gas flame. She turned to watch Pauline chop the vegetables and add them to a mixture of various types of greens.

"Why do you think Kelley chose us, you and me?" Sarah asked.

Pauline shrugged. "I don't know."

"Personally, I don't know that we're that much alike. You're certainly a more outgoing woman than I am. Taller, darker. I wonder what attracted her to each of us."

"I don't know," Pauline repeated. "Perhaps she saw a need in each of us and thought she could fill that need."

Sarah rested her chin on her hand. "You could be right. I was alone and desperate for a job when she hired me. It was very easy for me to like her, even though I had no idea she was interested in me other than as an employee." Sarah laughed. "I was so stupid! She said and did things that should have given me a clue, but I never saw it." Sarah looked at Pauline. "Somehow, I have never seen you as needy."

"Then you would be wrong," Pauline said with a frown. "When I met Kelley, I was quite alone. Very lonely. I had been involved in a bad relationship years before. After that I didn't trust anyone to be close to me. I mean, I did occasionally go out on a date, but I had already decided in advance that even though I might sleep with them, I couldn't trust them. I didn't trust Kelley after the first time we were...together."

"Really?"

"When I awakened the next morning she was gone." Pauline shrugged. "I thought she had simply slept with me and that was all she really wanted. It turned out she had only left to get breakfast, but I had doubted her. I was very angry at the time."

"I was angry at her, too. I didn't know what was happening between us. Suddenly, she disappeared and I didn't see her for two weeks. I went to her home to confront her, but it turned out much differently than I had originally planned. That was when I knew I was in love with her."

"Sometimes I thought she was terribly insecure, deep down inside. It was as if she wanted me to be the first to say I love you. Once she had that acceptance, she felt free to move on."

Sarah thought about what Pauline was saying for a moment. "Perhaps you're right. I've never thought of Kelley as insecure, but maybe she was and needed for both of us to commit to her first."

"In our own way, we both needed her to take care of us and she did. We trusted her so much we never questioned anything she did. We each simply accepted that she loved us as much as we loved her. It was enough."

"Until she was gone. Do you think she gave any thought to what would happen when she retired?"

"I don't like to think about that. I suspect one of us would be divorced," Pauline said with a frown, "and I suspect it would have been me. You are younger and still very beautiful. She lived longer with you and you had a family together. Those were things I could never give her."

Seeing the sadness in Pauline's eyes, Sarah stepped closer to her and wrapped her arms around her. "She loved you," she whispered. "Don't ever doubt that."

As Pauline held Sarah in her arms, she felt a sense of peace wash over her. "Will we always have this sadness between us?"

"I don't know. It will always be there to some degree, but it will lessen a little every day, I hope." Sarah released Pauline and checked the pots on the stove. "I think our dinner is almost ready. I don't know where anything is, so I'll let you set the table."

A few minutes later both women settled into their chairs. Sarah filled Pauline's plate and then her own. "Would you care for some wine with dinner?" Pauline asked.

Sarah looked at her and laughed out loud. "After the last dinner we had with wine, I think I'll stick to water or tea to avoid further embarrassment."

"You were irresistible," Pauline said.

They ate silently for a few minutes before Sarah spoke. "When did you begin writing? The first time."

"Many years ago. I never intended for anyone to read what I wrote. It began as a kind of therapy. Jolie convinced me to send a manuscript to a publisher. I thought if nothing else, I might get back some constructive criticism. I never dreamed they would accept it."

"Why did you need therapy?" Sarah asked between bites of food.

Pauline pointed to her plate with her fork. "This is excellent. You will have to give me the recipe."

"Thank you, but you dodged the question."

Pauline thought for a minute. "When I was younger, and quite naïve, I fell in love. Or at least I thought I was in love. She was not much older than I was, but she was experienced. I was so infatuated with her that I ignored the way she acted, the way she treated me. I know now that what I thought was making love was actually nothing more than having sex. When she announced she was leaving Quebec and moving to Vancouver I was certain she wanted me with her. Like the foolish young woman I was, I followed her."

"How long were you together?"

"Two or three years. She had a very bad temper and the move to Vancouver didn't turn out to be the new beginning she believed it would be. When she was angry, she drank. The last night I was with her, she..." Pauline stopped and cleared her throat.

"I'm sorry. I didn't mean to bring up bad memories," Sarah said. She reached across the table and took Pauline's hand. "You don't have to tell me."

"No. I want to. You have a right to know. She beat me that last night. She'd hit me before, but never like that. She was out of control. When I woke up later, I was in the hospital with a broken arm. My nose was broken and I had a fracture of my cheekbone. Although I don't remember, the doctor said I may have been raped as well. I had some tearing and bruising in the vaginal area. He said they had used the rape kit and documented my injuries. Of course they found nothing."

"Was she arrested?"

"No. Her friends bought her a ticket back to Quebec and convinced me to not press charges. After I was released from the hospital I never saw or heard from any of them again, except Jolie. That is why she is so special to me."

"She loves you, doesn't she?" Sarah asked softly.

"Yes. I love her as well, but she knows I am not in love with her. There has never been anything intimate between us." Pauline took a deep breath. "When I returned from Boston, after we spread Kelley's ashes, I was distraught and confused. I didn't understand what I was feeling for you. Jolie and I went out with some friends. I'd had a few drinks, but I wasn't drunk. When she took me home I kissed her and offered to sleep with her because I knew she'd wanted me, but she turned me down. She knew I wasn't in love with her. I would have used her to forget Kelley, at least for a few hours. That is the closest we came to being intimate."

"She's a good friend."

"Yes, she is. Anyway, while I was recuperating from my beating, Jolie suggested I write about it so that maybe I could come to grips with it. Understand why it had happened. And that is how I began writing. As therapy."

"Is that why you started writing again after Kelley died?"

"I suppose. I gave up my therapy after I met Kelley. I was

happy and didn't need it."

"Did Kelley want you to stop writing?"

"I don't think it mattered to her either way. She had never read much lesbian literature."

"She used to laugh at me because I read quite a bit of it. I still do. I'm ashamed to say I'd never read anything you'd written until recently. I enjoyed it, but it did make me cry in a few places because I could feel the pain you were feeling. I mean what the main character was feeling. I'd like to read your other books sometime."

"I will give you copies before you return home."

"Now that I know they were therapeutic maybe I will be able to understand you better."

"Perhaps. Tell me about your first marriage."

"Wow, that is going back a ways. I married Clifford Turner when I was very young. Just out of high school. I worked and got him through college. He was hired for a very good position with an investment company and we lived comfortably. I worked until my son was born, but mostly at minimum wage jobs because I had no real skills. It was never a good marriage. It was everything my family expected me to have. A husband with a good job, children, a nice home, a new car. I spent my time working with the PTA, volunteering at the children's school, and attending social events with Cliff. I was pretty naïve and certainly inexperienced sexually. I believed most of what Cliff told me. That was right up until the time I caught him with his secretary." Sarah laughed. "That sounds like what I've seen in a dozen movies. Anyway, Cliff said he didn't want a divorce because of the kids. I continued to live with him, but he simply couldn't stay away from other women. Finally, I filed for divorce. His lawyer was better than mine and I walked away with nothing more than child support. Since that's based on income, Cliff left his job and decided to return to school. In essence, he no longer had an income and I had to return to work."

"That's when Kelley hired you?"

"Yes. She saved me from having to file for public assistance to feed my children."

"Did they see their father often?"

"He disappeared not long after the divorce. I have no idea where he is or even if he's still alive. It was hard on Cherish and Carl, especially Cherish."

"She's the one who hated Kelley?"

"Yes. She's come to grips with what her father did and my life with Kelley now. I wish she could have done it while Kelley was still alive."

"How would she feel if you met someone new and fell in love?"

"I don't know. I think she saw my life with Kelley as an aberration, temporary insanity maybe."

"And Emma?"

"She knew I liked Emma, but it never developed into anything serious. I don't know what she would have done if we lived together."

"Stay here with me this week," Pauline said.

"I'm not sure that would be a very good idea. The temptation might be too great and I'm not very strong when it comes to temptation."

"I promise I will not do anything to tempt you, Sarah."

"You do that by just sitting there."

"You mean you want me?"

"Of course, I do. What a silly question. Who wouldn't want you, Pauline? You're a beautiful woman."

"I have many flaws."

"Such as?"

"I cannot promise not to touch you, but I will not try to convince you to go to bed with me. I would like nothing more, but ultimately that has to be your decision. I promise not to pressure you. Please stay here with me."

"Let me think about it. When can you come to Boston again? You don't know me either. Or the life I shared with Kelley."

"Probably in a couple of weeks. I am training Suzanne to completely run the bookstore. I'm traveling more now to promote my books and will need to be away quite a bit. I would enjoy seeing how you live."

After they cleaned the kitchen and put everything away, Pauline drove Sarah back to her hotel. Sarah agreed to spend the remainder of the week with Pauline. Pauline escorted her to her room to pack. When Sarah placed the last of her clothing in the suitcase and closed it, Pauline said, "Are you sure this is what you want? It's not too late to change your mind."

Sarah brought her hand up and stroked Pauline's cheek. "I'm a big girl, Pauline. Take me home."

"I DON'T UNDERSTAND why you need to return to Boston so soon," Pauline groused three days later as she stopped at the short-term parking entrance near the United Airlines terminal at the Vancouver airport and pulled a ticket from the automated machine.

"When I decided not to sell my home in Boston, I discovered there were some repairs needed that couldn't be put off. As it turns out, there were more repairs than my contractor originally thought and I have to go back to discuss what work that will entail and whether it can be completed before winter comes."

"I'll miss having you with me, you know. Have you discovered my bad habits yet?"

"I think you've been extra careful to make me think you don't have any," Sarah quipped.

Pauline found a parking spot on the second level of the parking garage across the road in front of the main terminal. She swiveled in the seat and pulled Sarah into a fierce hug. "Don't leave me," she whispered. "I love you."

"I love you, too, Pauline. The next two weeks will seem like a lifetime," Sarah whispered back.

"Perhaps we can spend some time at the cabin while I'm there," Pauline suggested.

"I never thought I would use it again and sold it. I should start working my way toward the terminal, sweetheart."

Pauline took a deep breath and let it out through her mouth. "I hate this," she mumbled. "I really hate this." She walked to the rear of the vehicle and took Sarah's rolling suitcase out and pulled it behind her as they walked hand-in-hand toward the building. Pauline waited as Sarah checked her suitcase in and received her boarding pass.

"Did you bring your book?" Pauline asked when Sarah rejoined her.

"Yep. I'm all ready to go," Sarah beamed.

"Well, you don't have to look so damned happy about it," Pauline huffed.

Sarah leaned against her. "It's my way of dealing with how much I'll miss being with you," she said.

"I refuse to spend all my time in an airport saying goodbye," Pauline sighed as she wrapped an arm around Sarah's shoulders. "I'll make a decision about the store soon."

"It won't always be like this. I promise."

Before Sarah turned away toward the security line, Pauline brought her close for a final kiss. As she hugged her she said, "I'm in love with you, Sarah. I think I have been since I first saw you."

"And I'm in love with you, baby. See you soon," Sarah replied. "For the first time in two years I feel at peace."

"Call me when you get home so I know you're safe."

Sarah nodded and walked toward the security and customs gate. She glanced over her shoulder and gave a final wave before she cleared the area and walked toward her concourse.

Chapter Sixteen

"SUZANNE. CAN YOU stay after we close for a few minutes? I have something I'd like to discuss with you," Pauline said when she returned from the airport.

"Of course, Pauline. Have I done something wrong?" the young clerk asked.

Pauline laughed. "No, and I am not your school principal. You're not in trouble. In fact, what I want to ask you may be good news," Pauline said as she started up the stairs to her apartment. "Come upstairs after you close."

Nearly an hour later Pauline was drying her hands with a kitchen towel when there was a knock at her apartment door. She turned the volume on her television down before answering the door.

"Come in, Suzanne," she said. "Would you like something to drink? I have coffee, tea, and soda."

"No, thanks. I haven't finished my drink from earlier." Suzanne looked around the apartment nervously. In the four years she had worked for Pauline, she had never been inside the upstairs apartment.

"Please. Have a seat," Pauline said as she re-entered the main room carrying a cup of coffee.

"This is a nice apartment," Suzanne said.

"It's better now after all the renovations Kelley made to it." Pauline's eyes swept around the front part of the apartment, and she took a drink from her mug.

"You miss her, don't you?" Suzanne asked.

"Very much."

"She was a nice lady. I could tell by the way she looked at you that she was crazy about you."

"I was a lucky woman. But that's not the reason I wanted to talk to you, Suzanne."

Suzanne straightened her body on the couch which faced a large window overlooking the street in front of the bookstore. The television was on, but the sound had been muted.

"You've been with me for a long time," Pauline began. "I appreciate your loyalty."

"I love being around books. When I come to work every day, the smell of them makes me feel good."

"When Kelley passed away, in her will she left me this store and the apartment free and clear. There is no payment to be made on the property now other than the annual taxes. Now that I am writing again and don't have the financial concerns I once did about the store, I've decided to spend less time in Vancouver."

"You're closing the bookstore?" Suzanne looked as if someone had slapped her in the face.

"No, no," Pauline said waving her hands to calm Suzanne down. "I won't close the store. I didn't mean to upset you. I was hoping I could convince you to become my partner. Because it is paid for, it will cost you nothing. I need someone to run the business in my absence. If you agree, you will continue to receive your paycheck plus a raise for being the manager. And you may move into this apartment rent-free as long as you remain my partner. Think about it, and I'll have my attorney draw up the paperwork."

"Yes," Suzanne said quickly.

"Take a day or two to consider everything, talk to your family, or..."

"Yes! I will do it. It's what I've dreamed of most of my life." Suzanne covered her eyes and leaned back on the sofa, bouncing slightly in her excitement. "Oh, my God! I can't believe this! Alice will be so excited."

"Alice?"

"My girlfriend. We've been putting off getting married until she graduates from college. I hate where she lives because it isn't in a safe area."

"It's a beginning, Suzanne, but you will still have to work very hard. I will not be here most of the time. Our accountant will help you learn the recordkeeping system, and I hope you do better than I have."

"Alice is studying accounting. She can help me," Suzanne said. A bright flash on the television screen drew her eyes toward it. "Damn! Did you see that?" she asked, pointing at the television.

Pauline leaned forward and looked at the screen. She saw a news headline crawling slowly across the bottom of the picture of a reporter standing in the rain. Behind him a muddy field was littered with burning debris. The reporter pointed over his shoulder to the wreckage behind him as Pauline grabbed the remote for the television and increased the volume. "...according to flight controllers the cockpit crew declared an emergency after the plane was struck by lightning. Communication between the tower and the United Airlines flight was lost a minute later and the plane disappeared from the radar. What you see behind me in an Indiana field is all that remains of that flight. Early reports indicate there were no survivors." A tag appeared below the reporter indicating he was a reporter with a television station in South Bend.

"What is known about this flight, Jerry?" the reporter in the studio asked.

After a transmission pause, the reporter on the scene said, "All we know right now is that United Airlines flight 5216 originated in Chicago and was bound for Boston, Massachusetts. According to the flight manifest, there were a hundred and eighty-five passengers and crew on board. An NTSB team is scheduled to arrive within the hour, but weather appears to have been a factor in the accident."

Pauline dropped the remote and rushed into the bedroom to grab her purse. She emptied the contents onto the bed and separated the items until she found a slip of paper. Her hand was shaking as she sat on the edge of the bed and looked at the paper. Sarah had flown from Vancouver to Chicago on United flight 7488 and caught a connecting flight to Boston. United 5216. She stared numbly at the paper before it slipped from her hands and fluttered to the floor. "Sarah," she whispered as she covered her face with her hands and felt new grief wash over her.

PAULINE'S EYES FLUTTERED open a few hours later. The apartment was dark except for the dim lighting from the streetlights below her windows. She rolled onto her back in her bed and stared at the ceiling. She didn't remember falling asleep. All she remembered were pictures of Sarah's plane scattered over a field, the pieces still burning. She closed her eyes to shut out the scenes from the television as a new wave of grief crashed over her. When her tears began to pass, she sat up and swung her feet off the bed. The red numerals on her alarm read three-fifteen. Her mouth was dry and she carefully made her way into the kitchen. She blinked at the harsh light from the refrigerator as she reached inside and took out a bottle of water. She walked back into the living room and plopped down on the sofa. She was distracted by the blinking light of her answering machine. Seven messages. Pauline leaned her head against the back of the sofa, remembering she turned off the ringer on her phone so her time with Sarah wouldn't be interrupted.

She reached over to press the play button. She closed her eyes and a strangled sob left her mouth when she heard Sarah's voice. She would never see the way Sarah's face softened as she became aroused, feel the little goosebumps that rose along her body as she trembled under Pauline's touch, or feel the rush of hot breath against her ear as Sarah's body finally succumbed to the release of her passion.

"Hi, sweetie. Just wanted to tell you I love you again before I get on the plane. Two weeks will seem like forever. I'll talk to you in a few hours." A gasp left Pauline's mouth and she covered it with her hand.

The next three messages were blank, as if someone had called and changed their mind. Pauline's thoughts were interrupted by a hurried message.

"Pauline. Please pick up!" Sarah's voice begged. "I missed my flight in Chicago. I saw the news when I landed in Louisville. I'm all right, baby. A little shaken, but otherwise I'm fine. I should be back in Boston by midnight. I'll try again when I land. I need to know you're all right."

Pauline closed her eyes and listened to the final message as tears once again streamed how her face. "Why don't you answer the damn phone?" Sarah said. "I forgot to charge my cell before I left Vancouver and now it's dead. Please call me when you get my message. I have to hear your voice. I love you."

Pauline took the handset from the cradle and speed-dialed the number she wanted. The phone on the other end of the line rang several times without an answer. She leaned back on the sofa again and let it continue to ring. She didn't try to stop her tears when a muffled, half-conscious voice finally answered.

"Ha-lo,"

"I love you," Pauline said softly.

"Pauline? I've tried to reach you for hours. Are you all right?"

"I am now. We turned the ringer off while you were here."

"I missed my flight in Chicago because we were busy flying in circles waiting for a storm system to move out of the area. The only other flight available stopped at every town between Chicago and Boston. I only got home a couple of hours ago. I didn't mean to worry you, baby. I desperately need to hold you."

"I'll be there tomorrow," Pauline said. "I don't know the flight yet, but I'll take a cab to your house."

"Call me back when you know the flight number. I'll pick you up."

Pauline barely made the next flight from Vancouver to Boston three hours later. She fell asleep immediately and woke only to change planes one time. By the time the Alaskan Airline flight landed at Logan International Airport nearly eight hours later Pauline stretched and felt rested as she stood to exit the plane. She made her way through customs and waited anxiously for the official to examine her passport. Her eyes caught a glimpse of blonde hair outside the customs area and she gratefully took her passport and stuffed it into her shoulder bag. Her eyes never left the blonde hair in the group of individuals waiting to greet their friends and loved ones. As she stepped past the last person, Sarah's beautiful face beamed and she rushed toward Pauline who swept her into her arms and kissed her fervently.

"You feel wonderful," Pauline whispered as she tightened her arms around Sarah.

"Let's get your baggage and get out of here," Sarah said.

"I was nearly destroyed when I saw the news," Pauline said, taking Sarah's hand in hers.

"I called as soon as I could and was disconnected three times. Even the air phones didn't work because of the weather," Sarah said. "My alternate flight from Chicago took off and landed six times before we reached Boston. A regular milk run."

"I was terrified," Pauline said. A lump was forming in her throat. "I didn't want to believe I'd lost you so soon after finding you again. That would have been too cruel. I decided then that I was never going to leave your side again. You're stuck with me now, lady." She wrapped an arm around Sarah's shoulders and hugged her.

They waited for the luggage from Pauline's flight to drop onto the conveyer belt in baggage claims. Then Sarah led her to her car in short-term parking. As soon as Sarah backed out of her parking spot, she said, "Now you'll get a chance to see where Kelley and I lived."

"I can stay at a hotel if you'd prefer."

"Not a chance. I have plenty of room, believe me."

"THIS IS A wonderful old house, Sarah," Pauline said as Sarah gave her the grand tour.

When they reached to first floor Sarah asked, "You don't think it's too much for just two people?"

"I thought you lived here alone." Pauline said as she followed Sarah into the living room.

"I was...was hoping maybe you would consider living here with me," Sarah said, looking down.

"Is that what you want, Sarah?" Pauline's voice was low and raspy. "Are you sure?"

Sarah raised her head and looked into the misty blue of Pauline's eyes. "It's what I want," she said. She brought her hand up to caress Pauline's cheek. "I've never been more sure of anything in my life."

Pauline wrapped her arms around Sarah in a firm embrace. She kissed the top of her head and began moving her lips down Sarah's temple and cheek before meeting her lips in a gentle kiss.

"Mother, what the hell are you doing?" Cherish's voice

interrupted.

Pauline slipped an arm around Sarah's waist, refusing to completely break the contact between them when Sarah abruptly ended the kiss. "Perhaps you should consider announcing your arrival in the future," Pauline said. Her tone was an odd mixture of amusement and annoyance.

"You! Oh, my God, Mother! How could you? And with her!"

Sarah looked up at Pauline. "We haven't done anything...yet," she said with a mischievous grin.

"What are you thinking?" Cherish asked.

"I am thinking that what I do is none of your business, dear. I'm an adult. I don't answer to you or your brother where my personal life is concerned."

"Have you forgotten that Kelley betrayed you? With her?"

"Kelley betrayed me as well," Pauline said. "With Sarah."

"Pauline didn't know about us until Kelley died, Cherish. She has done nothing to us knowingly. I can hardly blame her for Kelley's actions."

Pauline looked down at Sarah before facing Cherish again. "I am in love with your mother. I have struggled with my attraction to her for two years and I refuse to fight it any longer. My only wish is to make her happy."

"Oh, please. You're only saying that because you're sleeping together," Cherish huffed.

"We have not been intimate with one another, but even if we had been, it is not your business. Kelley may have been willing to overlook the way you treated her, but I am not. I am hoping Sarah will agree to marry me and I would gladly accept you and your brother as my step-children. I am not the bitch you think I am and I'm hoping you are not the bitch I've heard you are. However, I do not seek your approval, merely your acceptance."

"You want to marry me?" Sarah asked.

"*Oui*. More than anything," Pauline looked lovingly at her. "I love you, Sarah. Will you marry me?"

"Yes." Sarah said, hugging Pauline tightly.

The two women looked at Cherish. "Do you have something you wish to say?" Pauline asked.

"Is there any coffee?"

The three laughed as the tension surrounding them broke.

"LET'S PACK A bag and go to Vermont. I need to see the sun come up," Pauline said when she and Sarah were alone again.

"Okay, but I'll need to make a reservation someplace."

"Let's just play it by ear. It's not the tourist season and we should be able to find something. Can we make it before dark?"

Sarah glanced at the clock in the hallway. "We should be able to make it if we pack really fast."

As they approached Stowe a few hours later Pauline asked, "Can we stop by the cabin one last time?"

"I don't know, honey. I don't know if the new owners are there. We wouldn't want to trespass."

"I have a hunch no one's home," Pauline shrugged. "Can't hurt to look. We can always say we are lost."

"It'll have to be a quick stop if we want to find a room for the night before it gets any darker," Sarah said.

Sarah approached the cabin slowly, but didn't see any lights on and no cars parked near it. Pauline leaned forward and looked up the drive. "Looks like no one's home. Let's take a walk around the deck."

"What if the owner shows up?" Sarah asked.

"We'll just tell them how much we admire their home."

Sarah parked under the deck. Pauline came around the car and opened the driver's door. She took Sarah's hand and led her up the steps to the deck. She pulled Sarah in front of her and wrapped her arms around her waist, taking a deep breath.

"I think it smells better now than it did two years ago," Pauline said. "The trees will begin changing color soon." She turned around and peered through the large window into the open dining and living room area. Sarah stood next to her. "Looks like they kept most of the old furniture," she sighed.

Pauline moved to the next window, gradually moving around the cabin. The last room they looked into was the master bedroom. Sarah joined her and held her hands up to the glass to see inside. "They've replaced all the furniture in here," she said.

"Do you like it?" Pauline asked.

"It's beautiful," Sarah said when she saw the elegant four-poster bed. A gauzy curtain draped from the top crossbars. "I never liked poster beds because most of them are too heavy and clunky, but this one is very nice. Comfortable looking and inviting."

"Would you like to try it out?" Pauline whispered into her ear.

"That's trespassing, Pauline. God! Can you imagine what the owners would think if they found two total strangers sleeping in their bed?"

"Perhaps they would feel like the three bears in the Goldilocks story," Pauline joked.

"Well, I have no intention of pretending to be Goldilocks. Besides, I hate porridge." Sarah laughed and took Pauline's hand. "Let's go before you get another wild idea in your head."

"I love you, Sarah," Pauline said. She pulled Sarah back to her and kissed her thoroughly. When the kiss ended Pauline brought Sarah's hand to her mouth and kissed it. "Hold out your hand," she instructed.

Sarah's eyes still looked hazy from the desire Pauline's kiss had created as she held out her hand.

"Welcome home, my love," Pauline said as she placed a key in Sarah's hand.

"What are you talking about?" Sarah asked. "I sold this place over a year ago."

"To me, through a friend. It holds a special memory for me. It was here that I realized I was in love with you. I want to make it our home."

"Were you here last winter?"

"This is where I wrote *The Far Side of Happiness*," Pauline admitted. "I talked with Kelley, too. I know that sounds like I've lost my mind..."

"I believe you. I spoke to her in Vancouver. It was more of a feeling than real."

"I felt the same thing."

Pauline hugged Sarah. "I am so in love with you, Sarah. When I thought I'd lost you, my life ended. Then I was reborn by the sound of your voice on my answering machine. I don't want to take the chance that I'll lose you again. Do you know my deepest secret yet?"

Sarah looked into Pauline's steady blue eyes and shook her head.

"I want to make love to you."

Sarah rested her head against Pauline's chest and took a deep breath. "I'm scared, Pauline."

"Of me?"

"No. Of myself." She looked up at Pauline. "I've never made love to any woman except Kelley. I knew what made her happy, but what if it doesn't make you happy?"

"Just holding you in my arms makes me happy. Nothing you do not want will happen. Let's go inside and I'll start a fire."

Less than an hour later Sarah was snuggled close to Pauline on the sofa, facing the fireplace. Pauline kissed the top of Sarah's head and held her close. "Are you comfortable?" she asked.

"Very. You make an excellent pillow."

After a long day, a long drive, a good meal, and a warm fire, it wasn't long before both women drifted off into a comfortable nap. When Sarah blinked her eyes open, the fire had burned down to softly glowing embers. She raised her head and took in the sight of Pauline's head resting against the cushioned back of the sofa. She reached up to brush a strand of hair from Pauline's forehead.

Unexpectedly, Pauline grabbed Sarah's hand and brought it to her lips.

"Did you sleep well?" Pauline asked, looking into beautiful green eyes.

"Sorry I flaked out on you," Sarah answered.

"We were both tired. Maybe we should get a good night's sleep."

Sarah stood and held out her hand to pull Pauline up. Pauline hugged Sarah and took her face in her hands. She leaned forward and softly kissed her. Sarah wrapped her arms around Pauline and caught her bottom lip between her teeth. When she released it Pauline brought their lips together once again, her tongue asking for entrance. As her hands moved down Sarah's body, her tongue caressed Sarah's, stroking along its edges.

"Let's go to bed," Sarah said when the kiss ended.

Pauline nodded and hugged her before turning away and stepping toward the guest room.

"Where are you going?"

"I thought perhaps you would be more comfortable if I slept in the guest room tonight."

"Is something wrong, Pauline?"

"Of course not, but we haven't slept together before and I don't want to rush you into anything."

"I want you with me tonight," Sarah said.

Pauline lifted her head to look in Sarah's eyes again. "Are you sure?" she asked.

Sarah nodded. "Aren't you?"

Pauline's eyes searched Sarah's face. Then she moved carefully toward her again, stopping in front of her and taking her face in her hands. Pauline brought her lips closer to Sarah's and kissed her softly. Sarah parted her lips slightly and invited Pauline into the warmth of her mouth. As Pauline's tongue slipped inside, the heat of Sarah's mouth engulfed her and ignited her desire. When Sarah's head fell back, Pauline slid her hands beneath Sarah's pullover to touch the warm skin as she lowered her mouth to trail kisses along her throat. She drew Sarah closer, caressing her body. "I may not be strong enough to stop, Sarah."

"I won't ask you to," Sarah said as their lips met in a crushing kiss.

Pauline took Sarah's hand and led her down the hallway toward the master bedroom, pausing along the way to press Sarah against the wall to steal another kiss. Once they reached the bedroom, Sarah began to undress, but Pauline stopped her. She tugged Sarah's blouse from the waist of her jeans and began to unbutton it, her eyes never straying from Sarah's. She touched the exposed flesh on Sarah's chest above her lacy bra and kissed the area as she pushed the blouse over Sarah's shoulders and dropped it to the floor.

Trailing her hands down Sarah's exposed sides, Pauline knelt in front of her, untying her tennis shoes and helping her out of them. Still on her knees she brought her body up and encircled Sarah's waist, hugging her as Sarah's fingers combed through her hair. She felt alive again and the feeling drove her on. Pauline looked up at Sarah as she unsnapped her jeans and pulled the zipper down. Her heartbeat increased when Sarah wiggled her hips slightly to let Pauline pull the jeans down her legs. Sarah stepped out of the jeans and kicked them away.

Pauline's hands covered Sarah's buttocks and drew her gently closer as she pressed her face into the panty-covered apex of Sarah's legs. She inhaled the scent of Sarah's arousal deeply, holding it in her lungs as long as she could before releasing a slow breath. Standing, she moved behind Sarah, leaving kisses along her shoulders and the nape of her neck as she released the clasp of Sarah's bra. She pushed the straps down Sarah's arm, capturing her full breasts in her hands as it fell away. "You are exquisite," she whispered as Sarah leaned back against her, covering Pauline's hands with her own. Pauline brought her mouth down and felt Sarah's heart beat beneath her lips. She lowered her hands into the waistband of Sarah's panties and felt her pulse quicken as her hands teased their way through the coarse, curly hair and reached the wetness covering Sarah's sex. "So ready to be loved again," Pauline breathed into Sarah's ear. She withdrew her hands and turned Sarah to face her as she brought her fingers up and ran them beneath her nose, taking in the scent of arousal as Sarah watched, her green eyes searching Pauline's face.

"I want you, Sarah," Pauline said. "I never thought I'd say that to anyone again."

SARAH STRETCHED AND rolled over in the bed gazing at the sleeping woman beside her. Memories of touching and being touched, being overcome with passion filled her mind. Exhaustion had been the only thing that stopped the lovemaking some time in the middle of the night. Pauline had forced all intelligible thought from Sarah's mind, leaving nothing but the exhilaration her body gave and received. She shifted on the bed without disturbing Pauline before she leaned over and teased the dark pink nipple that was so tantalizingly close to her mouth. A sound Sarah could only compare to an infant's mewling when hungry came from Pauline's mouth as she arched her back slightly. Sarah closed her lips over the hardened nipple and sucked it into her mouth. She ran her palm down Pauline's abdomen until her fingertips slipped into the warmth between her legs. Pauline's hand pressed against the back of Sarah's head to deepen the contact with her breast.

When the pleasure her body was feeling finally pushed Pauline's body over the edge, she cried out Sarah's name and collapsed onto the bed. "What a wonderful way to be awakened," Pauline gasped. "Tell me again that you'll marry me."

Sarah brushed damp hair away from Pauline's face. "As soon as possible," she whispered as Pauline pulled her down into a lingering, lazy kiss.

Two hours later, Pauline and Sarah snuggled close together overlooking the valley where they had scattered Kelley's ashes two years before. They had missed the sunrise, but the warmth of the mid-morning sun caressed them.

"We'll never know why Kelley did what she did, but because of her, I've been given a gift I never dreamed I'd have again," Pauline said.

"Her final gift to us was one another," Sarah said as a tear ran down her cheek. "Do you think she knew this would happen?" she asked, looking up at Pauline.

A hawk screeched in the sky above them as it rode the thermal updrafts in lazy circles. Pauline pulled Sarah closer and followed the hawk with her eyes. "Perhaps."

More Brenda Adcock titles:

The Sea Hawk

Dr. Julia Blanchard, a marine archaeologist, and her team of divers have spent almost eighteen months excavating the remains of a ship found a few miles off the coast of Georgia. Although they learn quite a bit about the nineteenth century sailing vessel, they have found nothing that would reveal the identity of the ship they have nicknamed "The Georgia Peach."

Consumed by the excavation of the mysterious ship, Julia's relationship with her partner, Amy, has deteriorated. When she forgets Amy's birthday and finds her celebrating in the arms of another woman, Julia returns alone to the Peach site. Caught in a violent storm, she finds herself separated from her boat and adrift on the vast Atlantic Ocean.

Her rescue at sea leads her on an unexpected journey into the true identity of the Peach and the captain and crew who called it their home. Her travels take her to the island of Martinique, the eastern Caribbean islands, the Louisiana German Coast and New Orleans at the close of the War of 1812.

How had the Peach come to rest in the waters off the Georgia coast? What had become of her alluring and enigmatic captain, Simone Moreau? Can love conquer everything, even time? On a voyage that lifts her spirits and eventually breaks her heart, Julia discovers the identity of the ship she had been excavating and the fate of its crew. Along the way she also discovers the true meaning of love which can be as boundless and unpredictable as the ocean itself.

ISBN 978-1-935053-10-1

Pipeline

What do you do when the mistakes you made in the past come back to slap you in the face with a vengeance? Joanna Carlisle, a fifty-seven year old photojournalist, has only begun to adjust to retirement on her small ranch outside Kerrville, Texas, when she finds herself unwillingly sucked into an investigation of illegal aliens being smuggled into the United States to fill the ranks of cheap labor needed to increase corporate profits.

Joanna is a woman who has always lived life her way and on her own terms, enjoying a career that had given her everything she thought she ever wanted or needed. An unexpected visit by her former lover, Cate Hammond, and the attempted murder of their son, forces Jo to finally face what she had given up. Although she hasn't seen Cate or their son for fifteen years, she finds that the feelings she had for Cate had only been dormant, but had never died. No matter how much she fights her attraction to Cate, Jo cannot help but wonder whether she had made the right decision when she chose career and independence over love.

Jo comes to understand the true meaning of friendship and love only when her investigation endangers not only her life, but also the lives of the people around her.

ISBN 978-1-932300-64-2

Reiko's Garden

Hatred...like love...knows no boundaries.

How much impact can one person have on a life?

When sixty-five-year old Callie Owen returns to her rural childhood home in Eastern Tennessee to attend the funeral of a woman she hasn't seen in twenty years, she's forced to face the fears, heartache, and turbulent events that scarred both her body and her mind. Drawing strength from Jean, her partner of thirty years, and from their two grown children, Callie stays in the valley longer than she had anticipated and relives the years that changed her life forever.

In 1949, Japanese war bride Reiko Sanders came to Frost Valley, Tennessee with her soldier husband and infant son. Callie Owen was an inquisitive ten-year-old whose curiosity about the stranger drove her to disobey her father for just one peek at the woman who had become the subject of so much speculation. Despite Callie's fears, she soon finds that the exotic-looking woman is kind and caring, and the two forge a tentative, but secret friendship.

When Callie and her five brothers and sisters were left orphaned, Reiko provided emotional support to Callie. The bond between them continued to grow stronger until Callie left Frost Valley as a teenager, emotionally and physically scarred, vowing never to return and never to forgive.

It's not until Callie goes "home" that she allows herself to remember how Reiko influenced her life. Once and for all, can she face the terrible events of her past? Or will they come back to destroy all that she loves?

ISBN 978-1-932300-77-2

Redress of Grievances

In the first of a series of psychological thrillers, Harriett Markham is a defense attorney in Austin, Texas, who lost everything eleven years earlier. She had been an associate with a Dallas firm and involved in an affair with a senior partner, Alexis Dunne. Harriett represented a rape/murder client named Jared Wilkes and got the charges dismissed on a technicality. When Wilkes committed a rape and murder after his release, Harriett was devastated. She resigned and moved to Austin, leaving everything behind, including her lover.

Despite lingering feelings for Alexis, Harriet becomes involved with a sex-offense investigator, Jessie Rains, a woman struggling with secrets of her own. Harriet thinks she might finally be happy, but then Alexis re-enters her life. She refers a case of multiple homicide allegedly committed by Sharon Taggart, a woman with no motive for the crimes. Harriett is creeped out by the brutal murders, but reluctantly agrees to handle the defense.

As Harriett's team prepares for trial, disturbing information comes to light. Sharon denies any involvement in the crimes, but the evidence against her seems overwhelming. Harriett is plunged into a case rife with twisty psychological motives, questionable sanity, and a client with a complex and disturbing life. Is she guilty or not? And will Harriet's legal defense bring about justice — or another Wilkes case?

Recipient of a 2008 award from the Golden Crown Literary Society, the premiere organization for the support and nourishment of quality lesbian literature. Redress of Grievances won in the category of Lesbian Mystery.

ISBN 978-1-932300-86-4

Tunnel Vision

Royce Brodie, a 50-year-old homicide detective in the quiet town of Cedar Springs, a bedroom community 30 miles from Austin, Texas, has spent the last seven years coming to grips with the incident that took the life of her partner and narrowly missed taking her own. The peace and quiet she had been enjoying is shattered by two seemingly unrelated murders in the same week: the first, a John Doe, and the second, a janitor at the local university.

As Brodie and her partner, Curtis Nicholls, begin their investigation, the assignment of a new trainee disrupts Brodie's life. Not only is Maggie Weston Brodie's former lover, but her father had been Brodie's commander at the Austin Police Department and nearly destroyed her career.

As the three detectives try to piece together the scattered evidence to solve the two murders, they become convinced the two murders are related. The discovery of a similar murder committed five years earlier at a small university in upstate New York creates a sense of urgency as they realize they are chasing a serial killer.

The already difficult case becomes even more so when a third victim is found. But the case becomes personal for Brodie when Maggie becomes the killer's next target. Unless Brodie finds a way to save Maggie, she could face losing everything a second time.

ISBN 978-1-935053-19-4-

Soiled Dove

In 1872, sixteen-year-old Loretta Digby fled her home in Indiana to escape an abusive step-father. Rescued from the streets of St. Joseph, Missouri by brothel owner Jack Coulter, she turns to the only work available. By twenty she became a much sought after prostitute catering to St. Jo's most influential men and dreaming of the day she can leave her past behind and start her life anew. Jack is enraged when he discovers his favorite employee's plan to leave. Bloody and beaten, Loretta is rescued by a young prostitute, Amelia Benson, and customer Reverend Cyrus Langford. Working with teacher, Hettie Tobias, who is traveling west for a teaching position in Trinidad, Colorado, Loretta and Amelia leave their former lives behind.

In the foothills of the Sangre de Cristo Mountains outside Trinidad, Clare McIlhenney has been struggling for years to make her father's dream of owning a cattle ranch in the west come true. Working with a few ranch hands and her foreman, Ino Valdez, Clare has slowly built the ranch over the last twenty years while overcoming everything that should have stopped her.

In the spring of 1876 Loretta and her friends arrive in the dusty Colorado town. Her first meeting with Clare McIlhenney is less than inspiring. When Clare is injured, over her strenuous objections, Ino hires Loretta as a temporary cook and housekeeper for the ranch. Over the next few months, Clare struggles with her unwanted attraction to the much younger woman, unable to forget the events of her past that led to the deaths of everyone she had been close to. Determined to never lose anyone else, Clare closed off her emotions and became a distant and disliked stranger to everyone around her.

Will Loretta be able to keep her past a secret and find a new life? Will Clare open herself up to loss yet again and put her own prejudices behind her? In a story of the struggles in a harsh and unforgiving time will the two women find peace at last?

ISBN 978-1-935053-35-4

OTHER YELLOW ROSE PUBLICATIONS

Brenda Adcock	Soiled Dove	978-1-935053-35-4
Brenda Adcock	The Sea Hawk	978-1-935053-10-1
Brenda Adcock	The Other Mrs. Champion	978-1-935053-46-0
Janet Albert	Twenty-four Days	978-1-935053-16-3
Janet Albert	A Table for Two	978-1-935053-27-9
Sandra Barret	Lavender Secrets	978-1-932300-73-4
Georgia Beers	Thy Neighbor's Wife	1-932300-15-5
Georgia Beers	Turning the Page	978-1-932300-71-0
Carrie Brennan	Curve	978-1-932300-41-3
Carrie Carr	Destiny's Bridge	1-932300-11-2
Carrie Carr	Faith's Crossing	1-932300-12-0
Carrie Carr	Hope's Path	1-932300-40-6
Carrie Carr	Love's Journey	978-1-932300-65-9
Carrie Carr	Strength of the Heart	978-1-932300-81-9
Carrie Carr	The Way Things Should Be	978-1-932300-39-0
Carrie Carr	To Hold Forever	978-1-932300-21-5
Carrie Carr	Piperton	978-1-935053-20-0
Carrie Carr	Something to Be Thankful For	1-932300-04-X
Carrie Carr	Diving Into the Turn	978-1-932300-54-3
Cronin and Foster	Blue Collar Lesbian Erotica	978-1-935053-01-9
Cronin and Foster	Women in Uniform	978-1-935053-31-6
Pat Cronin	Souls' Rescue	978-1-935053-30-9
Anna Furtado	The Heart's Desire	1-932300-32-5
Anna Furtado	The Heart's Strength	978-1-932300-93-2
Anna Furtado	The Heart's Longing	978-1-935053-26-2
Melissa Good	Eye of the Storm	1-932300-13-9
Melissa Good	Hurricane Watch	978-1-935053-00-2
Melissa Good	Red Sky At Morning	978-1-932300-80-2
Melissa Good	Thicker Than Water	1-932300-24-4
Melissa Good	Terrors of the High Seas	1-932300-45-7
Melissa Good	Tropical Storm	978-1-932300-60-4
Melissa Good	Tropical Convergence	978-1-935053-18-7
Regina A. Hanel	Love Another Day	978-1-935053-44-6
Maya Indigal	Until Soon	978-1-932300-31-4
Lori L. Lake	Different Dress	1-932300-08-2
Lori L. Lake	Ricochet In Time	1-932300-17-1
K. E. Lane	And, Playing the Role of Herself	978-1-932300-72-7
Helen Macpherson	Love's Redemption	978-1-935053-04-0
J. Y Morgan	Learning To Trust	978-1-932300-59-8
J. Y. Morgan	Download	978-1-932300-88-8
A. K. Naten	Turning Tides	978-1-932300-47-5
Lynne Norris	One Promise	978-1-932300-92-5
Paula Offutt	Butch Girls Can Fix Anything	978-1-932300-74-1
Surtees and Dunne	True Colours	978-1-932300-52-9
Surtees and Dunne	Many Roads to Travel	978-1-932300-55-0

Vicki Stevenson	Family Affairs	978-1-932300-97-0
Vicki Stevenson	Family Values	978-1-932300-89-5
Vicki Stevenson	Family Ties	978-1-935053-03-3
Vicki Stevenson	Certain Personal Matters	978-1-935053-06-4
Cate Swannell	Heart's Passage	978-1-932300-09-3
Cate Swannell	No Ocean Deep	978-1-932300-36-9

About the Author

Originally from the Appalachian region of Eastern Tennessee, Brenda now lives in Central Texas, near Austin. She began writing in junior high school where she wrote an admittedly hokey western serial to entertain her friends. Completing her graduate studies in Eastern European history in 1971, she worked as a graphic artist, a public relations specialist for the military and a display advertising specialist until she finally had to admit that her mother might have been right and earned her teaching certification. For the last twenty-plus years she has taught world history and political science. Brenda and her partner of fourteen years, Cheryl, are the parents of four occasionally grown children, as well as three and a half grandchildren. Rounding out their home are three temperamental cats, a poodle mix, and a Puggle puppy who snores like a freight train. She is looking forward to retirement in 2013 and a move back to Knoxville, Tennesse, and her roots. When she is not writing Brenda shoots pool at her favorite bar. She may be contacted at adcockb10@yahoo.com and welcomes all comments.

VISIT US ONLINE AT

www.regalcrest.biz

At the Regal Crest Website You'll Find

- The latest news about forthcoming titles and new releases

- Our complete backlist of romance, mystery, thriller and adventure titles

- Information about your favorite authors

- Current bestsellers

Regal Crest titles are available from all progressive booksellers and online at StarCrossed Productions, (www.scp-inc.biz), Bella Distribution and many others.

Lightning Source UK Ltd.
Milton Keynes UK

173134UK00002B/218/P